ON THE ROPES

RUBY SCOTT

The truth is: Belonging starts with self-acceptance. Your level of belonging, in fact, can never be greater than your level of self-acceptance, because believing that you're enough is what gives you the courage to be authentic, vulnerable and imperfect.

– Brene Brown

ONE

SAPPHY

The warehouse is dirty, debris and detritus are everywhere, and the exposed steel rafters holding up the roofing are old and tarnished. But none of that matters. Not to me. I'm not looking at what's been or even what's here now; the decay and neglect. I'm looking at what could be and all I can see is potential. More potential than what I could ever put into words.

However, I'm the first to admit it takes a bit of vision. The question is, will people be able to see what I see; through my eyes. I feel a daft grin spreading across my face and I'm bouncing on the balls of my feet as enthusiasm bubbles from my toes and upwards.

I glance in Maura's direction. Her gray eyes are taking in the room. She is tall and her wide stance roots her to the spot. She grasps her hands behind her back and raises her chin, taking in the expanse of brick and vaulted ceiling. The stance gives her the look of a Victorian master, both severe and compelling all at once.

I can't get a read on her, but that is nothing new. I've never been able to. Not really. She has the ability to hide her emotions better than most. It is what makes her good in business, or at least that is what she tells me.

The uncertainty makes everyone in the room work a little harder to please me, she'd explain with a smug, tight smile. I'm no different to everyone else she deals with.

I wait just a beat, but still she doesn't speak. Not a single word is uttered. My grin fades. I'm chewing the inside of my lip, as if I'm a dumbass teenager. What if she can't see this? What if all she can see is a derelict warehouse? I feel my stomach flip. My eagerness never allowed me to consider that she might be blind to my dream. Until now.

"So?" I say, deciding to break the silence, in the hopes she'll give me *something*.

She blinks once, twice. "It's a warehouse, Sapphy," she says in a very matter-of-fact manner, as if I can't see this.

I sigh. I should have known that she wouldn't see it as quickly as I had. Call it my vision, my dream, but it is more than that. I need this.

"Yes, it's a warehouse for right *now*. But imagine what it could be?" From the slow-blinking, I can tell that Maura isn't in the same book as me, never mind on the same page. "Tell me this building wouldn't make a perfect gym."

When I say gym, I'm not talking about a box standard gym. No, this would be a woman-only gym. A safe space to train and grow. I'll admit, I've blindsided her a little, because I've never come to her with any genuine proposition before. Sure, I've mentioned it in passing over the years, but I'm pretty sure she's always thought it was a pipe dream. One of these *if I won the lottery* type dreams. I was beginning to think the same thing until I saw this place.

Managing Evolve for the last four years has been fun. It's allowed me to both manage and coach since retiring from competitions. Lord knows I've earned enough silverware and trophies over the years to gain the respect of anyone interested in MMA, and I've made Evolve into the best martial arts gym in the state. But it isn't mine. I want something different. I can see it, feel it; and standing here today, I can almost taste it.

I can see the punch bags all down the far wall, and where the old plastic barrels are lying on their side, that is where the ring will be. A full size, twenty-foot ring, because this place is big enough to take it. Inhaling deeply, I can even smell the effort and anticipation of each punch thrown; the small, light thumps of quick, agile feet as they dance on the vinyl; squinting my eyes, I can see it all. Two women in the ring, with me balanced on the corner, shouting. Encouraging. A fizz of excitement fills my stomach. It's a world away from the heavy grunting, macho posing and sweat stains, which surround me at Evolve.

No, this would be different. It would still be competitive. It has to be competitive. But here it would be about competing with yourself and not just physically, but mentally too.

It's why I love training women. Of course, strength and speed matter, but with women it's more about strategy, forward planning, observing your opponent and identifying their weaker areas and their strengths. Using your mind and body together to outwit them.

There are very few women who want to spend time in an environment that starts and ends with testosterone loaded kings. It makes sense. MMA is a more masculine scene. I've noticed how toxic the culture can be from my years of being immersed in it. I want to change that.

Maura steps away from my side, venturing further into the huge, cavernous space. She walks carefully, as if she fears the building is going to collapse at any moment. I stand back, still trying to get a read on her.

"A gym?" she finally repeats when she turns back to me. "Do you really see a gym in this place?"

Maura isn't the first person I wanted to share my dream with, but the truth is that I need her. She's done well for herself over the years, and she comes from one of the best connected families in the state. I know she'd be able to invest without really blinking an eye.

"Yes," I answer honestly, leaning back against one of the metal pillars that support the roof. "I do."

Maura is silent and I have a feeling that deep down, she doesn't believe me. I need her to; I need her to see it the same way that I do.

I take a deep breath. "When I look at this place, I see hope. I see possibility, not just for a gym, but for the people who'll become members of it. I see women of all ages coming here, women finally having a place to work out in this city that is full of positivity and encouragement. They'll be able to build not only their confidence, but the confidence of others as well. It'll be a safe space for women to fall in love with everything fitness related and know that they're supported. Where they can believe they can achieve whatever they decide to set their minds to."

I'm not just trying to paint Maura a picture out of pretty words, I speak from the heart. I open my eyes, pushing off from the metal pillar. Dust flies down around me as I do, and I watch Maura take a step away from the resulting mess.

"I'm not getting any younger. I'm thirty-two. I've done everything I wanted to do professionally, and I've proven I can turn around a failing gym and make it thrive. I've even started bringing through the next generation of talent," I tell her. "I want to do one last thing. I don't know, call it my legacy." I hear myself sigh. "I want to pave a way for women to love this sport and themselves the way I do. When I first stepped foot in a gym, I found myself for the first time. You know that if I didn't truly believe in this, I wouldn't be pushing for it so hard."

Saying Maura is my only hope for an investment would be dramatic, but it's pretty close to true. She's one of the few people I know that has the ability to help me, plus...we have a connection. I haven't spoken to my actual family in years; my life knowing Maura nearly beats the time I'd spent within the confines of my family.

The gray hue of her gaze is still on me, and I think of her like a cat watching its prey. Here, I'm the mouse. I sigh as I look at her, stuffing my hands in the pockets of my jeans. "So, what do you think?"

Maura's silence hasn't unsettled me too much. She's quiet when she's thinking about something. The fact that she's thinking is good enough for me. When she does finally speak, it's in the voice she uses when she conducts business.

"How do you know that this business would be successful?"

I shrug. "I can't guarantee that it will, but Maura, when have I ever failed on anything when I've set my sights on it? Besides, I can feel this. Women want to feel strong and confident. They want a place where they can go and bust their ass to get better, a place where they're not judged. Isn't that what every woman wants? To improve themselves without fear of judgment? That's what we could turn this place into. It would be the safe space women need, where women realize just how truly powerful they are."

Maura stays looking at me for a few seconds longer. She blinks at me, once, twice. I feel anxiety rise in my chest. I'm fully expecting her to not buy it. God, I hate how she can be so unreadable.

When she speaks, I still don't know the direction that this is going to go. You would think about knowing her for as long as I have that I would have an easier time figuring her out. I don't.

"You might be right in theory, Sapphy. I think you have a solid foundation of an idea." She pauses, looking around, taking in the building itself. "But why here? What do you see in this place?"

"Hope." It probably sounds stupid, and I realize that as soon as the word leaves my mouth. I can't deny how I feel though. "I look in here, and I see all the possibilities that it could hold. Not only for me but for future patrons of this gym." I look back at her, our eyes meeting. "Tell me you don't feel it too, Maura."

Her eyes are on me, not so full of doubt now, but something else, something a little darker. "I feel something," she says, her voice dropping an octave.

Maybe approaching Maura was a mistake. Not a mistake... but a risk. I've always been a risk taker though, a fire walker. So, what's wrong with playing with a bit of fire? Especially when it stands in the way between me and my goals.

"Maura," I say her name, trying to match the octave that her voice took. "Are you willing to help me out? Help me realize what this place could be?"

I need to know before I continue to play with the fire that is Maura.

She drops her gaze. I feel a heaviness at the bottom of my stomach. She doesn't believe in me as I want her to, like I need her to. She looks around the warehouse a few more times, her nose scrunched, her lips pressed into a thin line. Finally, she speaks.

"I'll invest. But I'm not doing this out of the kindness of my heart," she says as she looks me up and down. "I expect to have my investment back within two years. Got it?"

I swallow as nervousness causes a flutter in my chest. I

knew her terms would be stringent, but the full investment back in two years is a tall order. When I'd done the figures initially, I'd based it on three years.

"Maura..."

She shakes her head. "No. If you believe in it that much, I expect you to turn a profit in that time. You'll need to if you want to keep it going and pay me back. On top of that..." She takes a step towards me and I immediately see where this is going.

I had a feeling deep down that it was going to end up like this. Maura and I have been like this since we met. I've always found myself fascinated by her. She's an enigma. Try as I might, I've never been able to understand her. I'm a moth to her flame.

We were much younger when we first met. It was wild and passionate from that first spark between us. Charles Hearst, Maura's father, had sponsored one of the first fight nights I was involved in and she'd been dragged along to accompany him. It was more to keep her out of trouble than anything else.

I still remember my arm being grabbed and held up in the air as the crowd went wild. It was so much to take in, but the one thing I remember clearly, as I tried to catch my breath, were those gray eyes staring up at me intently with a malevolent glint. I knew from that first moment she was dangerous and I wanted her.

I'd never felt such an intense attraction to anyone. Those eyes came to visit me in the changing rooms after the fight. As the other girls left, she walked straight over and kissed me with such hunger that I could feel her lips on me for weeks after.

"I'm Maura by the way," she'd announced, then turned and left me standing there wondering what the hell had hit me.

After that she'd turned up during my training session, and then again at a club I'd been at with friends. We couldn't keep our hands off each other. There was a fervor bordering on obsession. The intensity brought as many lows as it did highs, and the complete loop would start again. The spark, the fever, the ultimate high and then the crashing low, but for years I found myself in Maura's bed nearly as often as my own.

Abs, my oldest friend, calls what we have as toxic and fated. She swears she'll never understand why for someone so strong willed, I can never resist going back.

Maura takes another step towards me, moving slowly, once again like a predator stalking their prey. And once again, I'm the prey. A mixture of excitement and unease fills me.

"What else do you need from me?"

I'm leading her on and I know it. The game I'm playing is getting more dangerous. I can feel the flames nipping at my skin, singeing my hair. It's a warning that I need to step away. But I can't. I keep moving closer.

"Sapphia," she says my name in almost a singsong, a difference from the earlier octave change. "We both know what else I want from you."

I swallow as anticipation replaces the unease that settles in my stomach. I take a step back. My back hits the metal pillar I'd been leaning against earlier.

"What else could possibly be part of this deal?"

Now I'm just playing her game, watching as Maura grows more and more frustrated with me, annoyed that I'm making her work for what she wants. I may be the prey in this situation, but that doesn't mean I can't play a bit too, does it?

Maura stands in front of me, stopping with her body mere inches from mine. She leans forward, slamming her hand against the metal pillar I'm leaning against. Her solid build pins me against the beam.

If I want to, I can overpower her with ease. She may be taller, but my years of training make me quicker, stronger. I could lead this game on for hours if I wanted to, but I want to ensure that I have my funding.

Maura looks down at me through dark eyelashes, unblinking. The eye contact makes me squirm, as tingling excitement shoots through me. "Your body," she says through gritted teeth. Her words come out like a hiss. She reaches out, running her fingers over the strap of my tank top. "I want my money back, but most of all...I want your body whenever the urge takes me for the duration of the loan."

The feeling tickles my skin, making me shudder as I keep up the eye contact. "That's all you want?"

"I want your body and your attention whenever I say," she murmurs, her fingers moving further down my tank top until they reach the bottom, then slide under the cotton material, making contact with my bare flesh.

I shiver at her touch, my skin feels electrified. I don't have a clear idea of what I'm doing. All I know is that I'm doing everything in my power to achieve my goal, even if it means falling in too deep with Maura. But I'm not physically doing anything I haven't done before I reason with myself. I look over at her, noting how much darker her eyes are. They glaze over with lust, want and need. I feel smaller than I am, less protected.

Her hand continues moving, her cool fingers pressing against my warm skin. Pushing my tank top up, she exposes my pert olive breast. My nipple is almost quivering as she runs her thumb over it and I moan.

Even if I wanted to resist, I couldn't. I want her as much as she wants me. I want to lean up and kiss her, but I know better. I must wait until she lowers her mouth to mine. Only then will she allow me to take the lead. This is our tango. A movement of slow, predetermined steps where our roles are defined. I lead, dominate but make no mistake, yet the control remains firmly with Maura. It is her hunger for pleasure that drives our every encounter, and I am happy to quench her appetite.

The moment our lips collide, I bite back. My hands go around her waist, pulling her shirt from the waistband of her tight skirt. I want to feel her warm flesh. Pulling back from the kiss, I focus my attention on her neck. My warm breath against her skin excites her. Her hand drops to the outside of my loose sweatpants. She wants to see what I have for her. Pressing the loose material, she finds what she is looking for, the hard shaft she craves. I don't normally go out dressed to impress, but today, I was meeting Maura.

My hands make light work of the buttons on her shirt, pulling it apart to reveal full breasts hugged tightly within soft white lace. I can feel my heart beat fast, bursting out of my chest. Grabbing the white lace I tug it down, her breast spills out, warm flesh falls against my hand and I find myself mesmerized by a large full nipple, hard with excitement. I tug the lace of the other breast too, and smile as I sink my face into her ample cleavage.

My hands run down over her ass, down the backs of her thighs until I reach the hem of her skirt. I pull it up roughly. I've been here so many times I know how she likes it, and that is harsh and fast. To my delight, I find no underwear. I wasn't the only one who came prepared.

Placing my hand between the warmth of her legs, I press my fingers into the depths of her folds. My fingers slide as I realize how much Maura wants this. Perhaps she wants this more than she wants me, but right now I am too caught up in my own desires to care. My thumb strums over her engorged clit, releasing a moan that escapes between pants of heavy breathing. I sink my fingers into her sodden heat and suck her nipple into my mouth, teasing it between my teeth and tongue.

Fuck, she is ready. And so am I.

"Give it to me," she growls, her voice dropping in pitch.

I'd love to convince myself it sounded like begging, but I'm no fool. It's a demand.

I raise myself up to meet her gaze and her hands pull down my sweats in one fast movement to expose my tight black boxers; and the outline of what she desires. Sliding her hand through the slit of cotton, she grabs the dildo causing the straps to rub against my clit. I gasp. She smiles. The remains of the lubricant I placed around my clit this morning allows the soft rubber to glide against each side, and Maura knows it. She sees my eyes widen, hears my breath catch, as she pulls it free from its secret slumber. The rubbing sensation surges excitement through my body and I grab her ass cheeks, raising her off the ground in a small puff of dust.

Her legs wrap around me, and I turn, pushing her against the pillar. My breathing is hard. Pinning Maura against the pole, I release one ass cheek, while bringing my hand around to adjust the silicon shaft. The tip is already drenched in her juices but still, I take my time easing it in and out in small amounts, again and again until she pushes so hard against me that the full length slides inside her. My breath catches in my chest as I watch her eyes widen with pleasure. My hand returns to her ass, allowing more purchase for each thrust as I build on our already steady rhythm.

"Harder. Fuck me harder," the order spurts from Maura's lips in short pants of breath and I hear my own grunting as I oblige, pounding my hips into her. Every drive forward slides the silicon straps tight against the sides of my clit, as I ram deep into her core.

"Yes, yes. Don't stop!" she screams in my ear and I have no intention of breaking this momentum as my climax is building right along with hers. Sweat runs down my back, my tank top is sticking to me, but all I can feel is the throbbing pulse of my orgasm build as I hammer into Maura's dripping wet center. "Don't fucking stop!"

I thrust even harder, panting for breath, as I drive every ounce of energy I have left in me. My legs shake with effort and anticipation as the first waves of orgasm take hold, and then her legs squeeze tightly around me. In a vice grip her body tightens, her back pushing hard against the pillar. I stand my ground, forcing her to grind against me as she comes in an anguished howl and then in an instant she slackens, allowing her body to fall against mine. I take her weight. She feels heavier now. In that short, brief moment she gives herself to me.

I stand still, remaining inside her and I know she pulses around me but I can't feel it. My back is slick with sweat, my chest heaving with each breath. I was so close, but for now, my excitement has to be swallowed down.

"Be careful when you put me down, this place is filthy." Maura lifts her head from my shoulder, then blows a stray hair from her face.

Maybe I just imagined that scant few seconds of what almost felt like intimacy.

I release myself and lower her back down to the thick carpet of gray dirt and dust at our feet. She pulls down her skirt, flat hands smoothing out the creases on the shiny, green-ash colored material. I ease the dildo back into the folds of the tight boxers, and kick my leg out, then wiggle my hips so it finds a natural crease in which to lie. My hands are wet with Maura's pleasure. I wipe them on the sides of the boxers before pulling up my sweatpants.

I glance over and Maura is doing up the buttons on her shirt. With a deep breath she slides the hem of the shirt inside the waistband, the left side first, followed by the right and then the back. I pull the loose fabric of my long, black tank top over the front of my sweatpants, checking I too am tucked in. All of this happens in silence, and small clouds of dust seem to sparkle in the one shaft of sunlight from the skylights in the roof.

"I'll have the papers drawn up and all you need to do is sign them and get them back to me." Her hands brush against her skirt and then her shirt as she attempts to release the dust which clings.

"Should I get a lawyer?" I shove my hands into the pockets of my sweatpants. I can feel the dildo against my fingers. It feels good and try as I might, I can't stop myself from touching it.

Maura watches me and smiles. "My little warrior," she mumbles, kissing me gently on the cheek. "Don't waste your money. It's all very straightforward." In a shimmer of sunlit dust, she grabs her purse and heads for the door. "You can always drop the papers back to me *in person*."

With a quick turn of her head, she winks and gives me the same grin from the first night we met.

TWO

I keep refreshing my screen just to make sure what I think I'm seeing is real. Account Balance, $3,500,00.00. I stare again. This is happening. I'm grinning at my phone and bouncing on the balls of my feet. This is real, I keep telling myself, and inside my head I'm shrieking with excitement. I need to tell someone. My mind is in overdrive. Who can call to share my excitement? Abs, I could call Abs, after all she is my closest friend and she doesn't know it yet but I have big plans for us both with this money. I need her to be my right hand, my ally and conspirator to get this project off the ground.

My finger swipes away the money with all its wondrous o's and I bring up my contacts. Abs name appears first in my priority list but it is the second name that my finger is drawn to, the person I really want to be with to share this moment. Maura.

Technically, as she would tell me, we have already celebrated this partnership. We celebrated when I first took her to the warehouse, when I went into her office to sign the papers (multiple celebrations), and again when I went to collect the keys, but kissing her right now...it is all I can think about.

To hell with it, I'm going to phone her. My finger jabs her number to make the call before I can allow myself to change my mind and a fizz of excitement fills my stomach as I wait for the call to connect. It rings once, twice. The sun is spilling through the full-length window in my condo, and even though it's barely fifty degrees outside, I close my eyes and feel its warmth through the glass.

"Yes, Sapphy, what do you want?" Maura says curtly, pulling me out from my daydream in a snap.

"Hi," I hesitate a little. I want to say I'm excited and happy and I want to see you, but I can tell from her tone she is in business mode. "The money has come through. It's in my account and I wanted to—" *I want to come to your office and kiss you; to tell you about the contractor I've found; the color I was thinking of painting the outside of the building.* But I know it isn't what you want to hear. Instead I hear myself quell my enthusiasm, "to say thank you."

"Mm, okay," she replies automatically. I rub my toes against the edge of the rug. Disappointment has stolen my smile.

"Sorry, you're busy. I was just going to suggest I pop over in person and say thanks?" My voice raises at the end of my sentence. I'm trying to make my voice sound light and carefree, and if I make it sound like a question, she might say yes. There is no immediate answer, and I find myself willing her to agree.

"Sapph, I'm busy. I don't have time for this today."

"Tomorrow?" God, I hate when I sound needy.

"We'll see. I'll call you, okay. I've got to go."

Before I have time to say goodbye, the line goes dead. "That'll be a no then," I say to myself. In fairness, now the money for the development is in the bank I have more than enough to keep me occupied. I was up till the early hours of the morning going over plans and costings. Paperwork has never been my strong point, but I'm learning fast.

I look out over the wharf, watching one of the harbor cruise boats pull out of its berth laden with tourists wrapped up in warm jackets and sunglasses. I remind myself how lucky I am. If it weren't for Maura there would be no gym and this view, this condo? Well, that is down to her too, or at least her family's property company. I pay rent for it, but it's nothing close to the market rate. There was a time when I felt bad about it, worrying I was a *kept* woman. But as Maura said, it was lying empty since she had moved to her new penthouse apartment. This place was practically slumming it, compared to her five bedrooms and roof terrace with a pool, and besides it stopped her bitching about having to drive to the other side of town on the nights she chose to see me.

This arrangement works better for her and I can't complain. Think of it as a rent-controlled apartment, she had said, and who was I to argue with that idea. As long as I am paying my rent each month, I feel okay about it. I couldn't allow myself to stay here if it was any other way. It is very much like our entire arrangement. I call it an arrangement because I can't call it a relationship; because that isn't what it is. It is a mutually agreed arrangement.

Maura dips in and out of my life as she pleases. Sometimes I'll see her a couple of times in a week, sometimes I might not see her for a month. I don't fool myself into believing that I'm the only woman she spends time with because I know I'm not. Maura has several *partners*, such is her appetite, and we all serve a purpose. When there is a function to attend she normally has the poised and educated Valentina on her arm, when she wants to travel, then Faith and Hope (no joke) are the names who have popped up over the last year...and me? Well, I suppose I'm her bit of rough.

No ties, just fun; those are the rules and I have always abided by them. This arrangement suits me as much as it suits her, and it isn't like I haven't had an occasional one-night stand over the years. I don't do angst or drama, hence the reason I don't do relationships. I like my life to be simple. I had too many dramas when I was younger. Being the eldest daughter in a traditional Greek family isn't the ideal place to find yourself when you realize it's women that do it for you and not men.

I tried to hide it when I was young. I thought I might eventually understand why my friends became giggly and stupid whenever one of the football players walked by us in high school, if I just gave it time. But then a new girl arrived in 11th grade. Paula was her name. A name I'd written hundreds of times on the inside of my books next to odd heart shapes. A name I used to say out loud, like the most exquisite secret that could ever escape my lips.

Paula wore hoodies, combats and trainers. She hung around on her own. Just watching. I started investing heavily in plaid, trying to be just as broody. She was without any doubt the coolest girl I'd ever seen. Unsure of whether I wanted to be her or just be with her, when Paula joined the wrestling team, so did I. And two months later as she pinned me down in a cross face cradle, our nipples gazing, I knew my life had changed irrevocably.

That clinch sparked a rollercoaster of momentum, taking me from euphoria to misery; the climax of sexual awakening to the misery of family rejection. We were inseparable. Consumed. Nobody could understand what we had. How could they? Arguments at home escalated until all we did was shout at each other. Tears, arguments and angst, but through it all I knew I had Paula. Being awarded a wrestling scholarship to Penn State was my way out, and I grabbed it with both hands. It was going to be the start of our new lives together and for two years my life had everything I wanted neatly contained in it; love, happiness, future and friends. I'd come home.

That is what made what came next, so cruel. Paula's family were moving again, to California this time, and she was going with them. Her transfer to Berkeley had been agreed and dates set. I was the last to know or at least that is what it felt like. *I didn't tell you because you'd have tried to stop me.* Paula's words echoed. I wasn't enough for her. I wasn't enough for her to stay.

If it hadn't been for Abs and the strength of our friendship, I'm not sure what would have happened to me. That is what I think about when I think about those years, our friendship. If life has taught me anything it's that while I might not be a good enough girlfriend or partner or daughter, I am a good enough friend.

And I am about to be an even better friend if I can get her to agree to join me in this new adventure.

THREE

"Morning! I've brought donuts," I shout as I walk through the doors of the gym. My voice is drowned by the sound of a jack-hammer echoing at the far end of the warehouse. Two men in hard hats smile and nod. The irony of bringing donuts to the site that is soon to be a gym isn't lost on me.

Evidence of construction is all around as my vision leaps from the plans into form tangible change before my eyes. I know I don't need to, but I'm showing up every day. I have no expertise when it comes to building and I'm likely more in the way than helpful, but I want to be here. I want to see it grow around me.

Maura sends me texts requesting updates, emails demanding cost reports, messages insisting I send through photographic evidence of progress, but not once does she visit the site in person. I am at her beck and call. Her investment, her convenient lover, but I can't complain. After all, everything which is being built around me, Maura is enabling. If it wasn't for her, there would be no warehouse, no gym, no dream.

I stand back, looking at what will soon be the doors of my

gym. Right now, there is just a gaping hole in the concrete wall, waiting to be filled with the sleek glass which I picked out. Looking up, I see the men working up in the steel trusses of the building.

"Hey Sapphy." I'm interrupted from my thoughts by a voice coming from my side.

Looking over, I see Abs. My oldest friend and my first hire for the gym, or at least I hope she will be. We've always been close ever since we met on the wrestling team at college, but she taught me what genuine friendship was when she helped me pick up the pieces after Paula had left. From wrestling Abs moved onto boxing and I moved into Taekwondo. We've supported each other, rooted for each other in competitions and celebrated together with every victory. Abs was a gifted boxer, and she was blazing a trail for other women to join the sport. That was until the car crash which wrecked her hand so badly it ended her fighting career. But it crushed more than her hand.

I bore witness to how close it came to crushing her spirit too. But Abs is a fighter, and she had dragged herself back to fitness, and to a career in coaching new talent. I made sure I stood with her, supporting her in every step of that journey, just as she had done with me all those years before. I need her to be part of the team. Maura isn't a fan of that part of my plan...but it's something I won't budge on.

"Hey," I greet her back.

She offers me a cup of coffee. "I stopped off at Java Hut's. Thought you could use this. One large, black rocket fuel," she says with a smile.

"Because it's freezing out here or because you know I'm not sleeping?"

I haven't gotten a full night's sleep since Maura agreed to invest in this project. Excitement keeps me awake each time, planning more and more for the gym. Each day, I see my dreams shift and take a new form as other ideas come to me at night. Abs knows more about these ideas than anyone else, even more than Maura. There have been too many late nights over the last few years where we've sat with a beer and I've droned on about 'if I had my own place.' Well, now, I have and Abs is here to share my excitement.

"Both." She laughs and I laugh along with her. "I brought you a muffin as well because I bet you haven't eaten, have you?"

I shake my head and laugh. Abs knows me well. Probably too well.

My watch vibrates and pings. I tap the face and another message for Maura pops up on the screen. It was the third this morning. When she's not demanding updates over text messages, she's demanding that I appear in her office as quickly as possible. She says that she wants a 'verbal' report, but really, she just wants me on my knees in front of her, ready to please her at a moment's notice.

I haven't told Abs about my arrangement with her, knowing that she'll frown on it. Maura and Abs don't like each other. They never have. Abs can't understand my attraction to Maura. She thinks Maura just uses people and then tosses them aside when she has had enough. Maura thinks Abs is jealous of me. I have to stifle a laugh whenever Maura mentions it because I know Abs wouldn't give her the time of day, never mind anything else. The less Abs knows about Maura's involvement, the easier life is for all of us.

Pulling myself out of my thoughts, I turn to look at Abs. "Want a tour?"

She looks around us, likely taking in the dust, wooden boards, stray wires, and still visible metal pillars. "I think I see everything pretty well, Sapphy." She laughs.

"Not like that. I mean, do you want to see where everything's going to be?"

Her features soften and she nods. "Yeah. Gimme the tour. Let's see firsthand what this vision of yours is all about."

"You'll need one of these."

I toss her a hard hat, like the one I'm wearing, but hers is yellow to my white. I smile at her before turning and leading the way through the construction, doing my best to step carefully over stray tools and materials. I'm trying to stay out of the way of the workers who've been nothing but angels in putting up with my far too detailed interest in everything they do. I stop towards the right of the doors.

"This is where the reception desk is going to be. Through that door will be the front office." I turn and point towards the left. "I'm keeping the reception area fairly light and basic because I don't want to give up too much space from the main gym."

Abs snorts. "What? The size of this place and you're worried about giving a few extra square feet to the reception area? First impressions count."

I shrug. I know she is right, but it is the gym space which excites me the most and I don't want to waste time and energy here. Plus some hipster types who are moving into the area like a bit of that thrifty, grunge look. At least that is what I am telling myself in trying to keep the costs down.

I take a few strides forward to where the start of a timber framework is being constructed.

"Down here," I say, pointing to a second large vaulted area off the main warehouse, "is going to be three studio spaces for classes."

"Classes?" Abs echoes with a confused look.

I knew this might throw her off course a little. Abs is all about boxing, the ring, the bags, but we need more than that to make this place viable.

"Yeah, I want to ask Logan to join the team. Her expertise

could be a real asset and the whole Krav Maga, self-defense angle could serve us well. So she'd need a studio for that."

Abs grunts and gives a slight nod. "I thought you were about to tell me I'd have to train in Zumba," she teases. "I suppose you're right and having Logan on the team makes sense. Have you asked her yet?"

"Not yet. I need to know you are okay with all this before I go there."

As we step forward, I lift my arms with a flourish to present the main vaulted area.

"And here is where the proper action will take place. There will be a full size ring in the center and down the far wall," I point to the furthest away wall, "will be the bags and speedballs."

Twisting on the ball of my foot, I point in the other direction.

"And here I'm looking at getting some cardio equipment and then have the weight stacks with a free area for mats and skipping just behind." I pause, letting my arms slide down to my side. "What do you think?"

Abs doesn't have to say it, I know what she's thinking. I'm really dreaming big, aren't I? A full size ring and the place is huge, it will take a huge membership to fill it. No, to pay for it. But in my head I can see it filled with people. I turn with an expectant look. Can she see it too?

"If anyone can pull this off, it's you!" She grins.

"It'll take time, but I really believe we can make this work... if you'll help me?" I screw up my face with a little trepidation. "Will you? Help me?"

"As long as you don't expect me to teach Zumba or Jazzercise," Abs raises her hands in an old-fashioned variety show kind of way, "then I'm in." She laughs.

That's the thing about Abs. She always makes me laugh no

matter how stressed or nervous I get, especially when things aren't going my way and that can be often.

We wander through the rest of the building and I show her where the locker rooms and showers will be before we walk up the set up metal steps on the sidewall of the main gym.

"There will be a new glass front put on both rooms. The first is your office and I'll take the larger one that backs up towards the corner," I say, smiling.

Abs let out a long, low whistle before screwing up her face and asking, "How are you paying for all this? It must cost a bit, isn't it?"

"Mm, a bit. I got investment." Before she can ask any more questions, I distract her. I need Abs on board and letting her know Maura is behind this will not help my cause. "Now we are a little higher, you get a better view of the gallery area that will go above the studio's and locker rooms. I'm getting the construction guys to make it into rooms. I thought we could get in a physio, or maybe a massage therapist. We can even get the guys to link it to the back entrance that links onto K Street."

Abs's eyebrows rise in surprise. "You're going all out. I'm assuming we get staff discounts? Next you'll be telling me you're squeezing in a *day spa* right behind the boxing ring." She giggles.

I knew that would distract her.

"Okay," I say with a smile, "We need to sit down and work out how many people we'll need to hire and get interviews arranged because some might need to give notice before—"

"Excuse me ladies." Ray, the head contractor, is leaning against the door frame with his hard hat in his hand, wiping his brow. "I have a question if you don't mind me interrupting."

"I hope we have an answer." I grin. Before he opens his mouth to ask, my phone buzzes wildly in my pocket. At first, I reach down and quiet it, but it starts up again, almost immediately. I sigh, turning to look at Abs and the contractor. "Give me a minute and I'll be right back," I say, wandering through to the next room, which will eventually become my office.

They both nod and I pull my phone out of my pocket. One glance at the screen tells me I missed two calls from Maura, and I curse silently to myself. That's never a good thing. I call her back immediately, and she answers after the first ring.

"About time," she snaps through the phone. I wince.

I've never been *scared* of her—per se, but Maura is a woman that it is best not to disappoint, plus she has the power to snatch all of this away. I have come too far for that to happen, so it makes sense to stay on her good side.

"Sorry," I mutter into the phone. Being this submissive feels out of character to me...but if it keeps her happy, I can cope. "I was talking with Abs and the contractor."

When I mention Abs's name, I hear her scoff on the other end of the line, but she says nothing more. She moves past it. "You need to pay more attention to your phone, Sapphia."

I cringe when she uses my complete name.

"I know."

"Anyway, how is it coming along? Are we still on schedule?"

I nod, even though she can't see me. "Yes," I answer. "Actually, the contractor was asking me a few questions. I should probably go back—"

She doesn't let me finish. "Come see me. I need an update about construction and your business plan."

"Maura."

"Sapphy, I said I need an update." Her voice is sharp, and I know I can't argue. I also know that Maura isn't really looking for an update. She wants the other part of her payment plan.

"Now? Can't this wait?"

"Would I be asking if it could wait?" she snaps once more.

"Right. Alright. I'll be straight over." I sigh as I hang up. It is not that I don't want to spend time with her, but right now I'm reluctant. My excitement is here on this site.

I walk back over to where Abs and the contractor are speaking, and Abs smiles when she sees me. "There you are. Ray here was just asking me—"

I cut her off. "Abs, Ray, I'm really sorry. I have to go real quick. There's an errand I forgot about, and if I don't go now—" I raise my arms and shrug as if I have no choice. "I should be an hour, tops. Ray, can you hang on until I get back?"

"Sapphy, what the...are you just up and leaving?" Abs's eyes narrow in my direction.

I can't tell her where I'm going, but I don't want to lie to her either. Mentioning Maura's name would just stir the hornet's nest.

"I'll be as fast as I can, I promise. You know I wouldn't bail unless I had to." I smile apologetically.

"Sapphy, really? What am I supposed to do? You couldn't wait just five minutes?"

I make the most apologetic face I can, hoping Abs understands. "I really can't," I tell her softly. "But I'll be right back." I turn to look towards Ray, an uninvolved audience member of the sideshow that is my life. "Whatever your question is, you can ask Abs and I trust whatever answer she gives."

Her eyes widen. She looks between Ray and me. "Sapphy! Don't you dare put that much pressure on me."

Reaching out, I squeeze her shoulder. "Seriously, I trust whatever she says. She's my second in charge."

Before Abs can object again, I rush out of the building. She'll forgive me for it, or at least I hope she will.

FOUR

I pull into the parking lot of Maura's office building and step inside. It's warm and sleek; dark wood and burgundy decorate the area, with modern leather chairs in the waiting room. I walk up to the desk where a petite blonde with a bun sits. She looks up at me with pale pink lips and smiles. "Miss Adamos, nice to see you again. Miss Hearst is expecting you, please go on in."

Of course she is. I smile and give a small 'thanks' to the receptionist before stepping into Maura's office. It's just as sleek and polished as the reception area, with the same dark wood and burgundy hues. Her desk is large, taking up a good portion of the room. The walls are lined with fancy art. Expensive and impersonal.

When she sees me, Maura smiles. "You got here quick," she says before tacking on, "good." I'm rewarded with a large bright smile which melts my frustrations about being dragged off site. She closes her laptop, pushing it to the side of her neatly organized desk.

"I aim to please."

"How's everything coming along?" she asks, but she doesn't

need to. Between the progress reports and photographs I've been sending through, she is pretty much up to speed. The way we are smiling at each other, we both know why I'm here and it has nothing to do with contractors. I walk to her desk and sit on the corner. I wish I could say I'm looking sexy. In another situation, with someone else, I might be, but this feels contrived and I likely look like an uncomfortable gargoyle.

"Things are going well. The work on the roof is complete. The supporting beams for the gallery area above the studios are in place, too. They're onto the studwork for the studio's and reception. You'd be impressed—if you came down," I say, looking at my hands perched neatly in my lap.

She looks pleased, offering me a satisfied nod. "Good, good. It seems we're right on schedule. I'll wait until the place is further along before I visit. I had to send my skirt back to the dry cleaners twice after last time to get the grime out."

The memory of that last visit sends a twitch through my core. I wasn't expecting to be here today so I'm a little less prepared, but it won't interfere with our fun. Maura is a gorgeous woman. From the first moment we met I was attracted to her, and that has never waned. If anything, she's only grown more attractive with age. I make it sound like she's old. She's not. She's a year older than me, so thirty-three this year. Her features are fine, her neck long, and there is such depth to those gray eyes.

But it's her charisma which really draws people to her...and makes it impossible to pull away. Walking around the desk, she stops in front of where I sit, legs wide and open. Sliding between them, her hands come to rest over my thighs, excitement rushes through me as her heat radiates through my leggings. A slow smile comes over my face as her fingers run upwards, coming to a stop at the apex of my desire. I swallow, my eyes fluttering closed for a second. *Just slide your hands down, please.* My clit throbs, desperate for attention. She follows the seam of my leggings down, increasing pressure until she hits the precise spot. Three fingers slide over the lycra material in quick, short repetitive movements causing me to bite my bottom lip.

"Oh Sapphy, I don't need to ask if you are looking forward to this, do I? I can feel the answer," she whispers in my ear. "Do you like me teasing you?"

I nod meekly.

The blinds to her office are open, offering an unrestricted view of both the reception and the cute blonde behind the desk who is busy typing. Our bodies are partially shielded by a high-backed chair, but as her hand slips down the inside of my leggings, my look of shock is clear for all to see. In one slick movement, Maura reaches behind me with one hand while the fingers of the other slide defiantly over my clit. The blinds close with a whirr as I realize she has hit the remote on her desk.

"Do you want to fuck me, Sapphy? Because I sure as shit want to fuck you." Her smile grows ever more wicked. "Strip for me?" Releasing her hand from my leggings, she lifts her fingers to her mouth. They are coated in my juices and my breath hitches as I watch each of them slide into her mouth to be sucked clean; one by one. She takes one step backward and slides her hands down the sides of her skirt and then grabbing the hem she shimmies it upwards, revealing black lace panties.

I edge off the desk and slide my own hands into my leggings, running them down my thighs, removing my clothing in the process. I can't take my eyes off Maura as she slips beneath the lace to touch herself. I grab my tank and sports bra pulling it over my head listening to the groans Maura makes as her fingers go deeper. I close the distance between us and place my hand over hers with only the lace between us as she fucks herself.

Chatter comes from the direction of the reception, but rather than subdue our desire, it increases it.

"I want to watch you," my voice is low but urgent.

I lift Maura, placing her on the edge of the desk, with her fingers still deep inside. My thumbs hook into the lace of her panties and pull them down. The sodden gusset gleams as it lowers. She kicks it to the side and leans back on the desk, pulling her legs up and wide. A heel at each corner. I watch as her fingers slick with readiness, pull back to circle her clit and then dip down again. I touch myself as I watch her fingers gathering speed. She comes quickly and smiles at me.

"Bend over my desk," her order is firm, as she slides off the desk, "do not make yourself come. I want to do that." I pull my hand away and do as I'm told. The wood of the desk feels cold against my nipples. I feel her body behind me, her feet kick my legs wider apart and the cold air against my center, tingles. "I'll never grow tired of this Sapphy," she says as her long fingers push through my heat and into my core.

A hand pins me to the desk and I gasp as fingers roughly penetrate me. I can't move and I don't want to move. Each thrust is purposeful, masterful, and I groan as her rhythm relentlessly pounds deep into my center. I feel the flick of her thumb as it leaves my ass cheek to join her fingers. The weight of her body rides hard against her hand and I feel it ram deeper still into me.

"Fuck yes, Maura," I whisper my cheek hard against the coolness of her desk.

"I can't hear you. Are you asking me to stop?"

"No," I scream as I feel the first tingles of orgasm take hold.

"Louder," she orders.

"Keep fucking me, please," my voice is strangled as my orgasm crashes through my body in violent spasms and moans.

Shudders continue as I feel my release trickle gently down the inside of my thigh. I sink into her desk, spent and sodden.

"Good girl," she whispers, kissing my back. "Good girl."

When I straighten up, I'm unsure if my legs can hold my weight. I almost wobble but then jump when the phone rings. To my amazement, Maura answers in the most casual of tones.

"Yes, okay. Tell her to take a seat, I'll only be a couple of minutes finishing up with Sapphia."

Maura raises her hand to my mouth and slides in a wet finger. I suck hard, tasting myself.

"I'm only sorry we don't have more time." Her free hand slides over my naked body and then landing on my nipple, she roughly tweaks it. "Now get dressed. My next appointment is here."

I dress with haste, while Maura turns her attention to the laptop and I have barely pulled my tank over my head when she opens the blinds.

"I'll call you when I want the next update. And Sapphy— next time come packing."

I'm smiling when I leave her office, and the receptionist almost giggles as I walk past.

FIVE

I'm learning how to manage Maura better so I'm not having to take time off site during the day. I offer to meet her for drinks after work and this more than satisfies her as our sessions are that much longer.

At the gym I watch as the building springs up around me, watching as my vision comes to life. Studwork fleshes out rooms and doorways; possibilities become reality. Brick walls are scoured, treated, sealed and painted. A full concrete screed is poured and leveled in the main area before they apply a rubber surface. It's turning into a proper gym right before my eyes.

Today the equipment begins to arrive, starting first with the ring. A crew of eight follows the lorry laden with the metal frame, wooden boards, mats and ropes. A cute blonde with a tool belt and cargo pants seems to direct the efforts. I'm admiring her expertise when Abs sneaks up behind me.

"If you'd told me we were going to have this much excitement today, I'd have arrived earlier," she teases before running up the stairs to her office to dump her stuff.

I'm still watching them work when Abs reappears.

"Aren't the studio floors being laid today?" she asks, breezing past me with a pile of CV's in hand.

"What? Oh yeah. They called to say they're running late," I say absently with a wave of my hand.

"I still can't believe how much one of these sprung floors cost. If you hadn't been so set on having the whole yoga, pilates thing, you could have saved a fortune. Logan said she was fine with just a standard floor and mats. I'm ordering them later. The mats, I mean. The rep from the equipment company is coming by about 2 pm. Do you want to be there?" Abs looks at me expectantly and I nod.

You want a yoga studio? was her response when I told her about my plans. Abs has never been able to hide her feelings about anything from me. To be fair, few people would think about me and yoga in the same breath, but I've done my research, and it makes sense both financially and from a health perspective. Yoga is popular and according to what I'd read, it centers attention and sharpens concentration. Neither of them could argue with those benefits. It may not seem like it, but it's a perfect fit.

"Are you joining me for this morning's interviews?" Abs waves the pile of CV's in the air again. "We've got part-time receptionists first, and then Logan is coming in at about 11.30 to help me choose instructors."

"Yeah, I'll sit in until Logan gets here. It'll be good to have her working with us."

Having Logan in today was the first time that we'd have the core team together. Abs had taken to the deputy manager's role like a duck to water, and I knew that having Logan there to support her would make our entire structure stronger.

Logan and I have been friends for a few years now, and it had been quite a journey for both of us. She wasn't interested in the competitions, and unlike Abs and I, she hadn't come from a boxing or martial arts background. Her journey had been a little darker. Logan's ex-partner had been pretty handy with her fists. MMA was a way for Logan to become stronger; protect herself; and gain some much needed confidence.

Training Logan had been easy, she was a natural, light on her feet, fast, agile and focussed. But, and there was a big but, she didn't have the killer instinct. What Logan has though is solid empathy and a need to help. So when she announced she wanted to become a Krav Maga instructor, I knew it was a perfect fit. I'd hired her to work with me at *Evolve*, and she was one of the best fitness trainers we had. Having her here as part of the team made sense. Good business sense.

My team is slowly coming together.

Hopefully, by the end of the day we'll have a couple of part-time receptionists that can man the desk when we are taking classes and a few more trainers. Given we've all been in the industry for years now, word has got around that we are hiring. All women, of course. Without having to spend a penny on advertising, we've been inundated with applications and many were keen to bring a client base with them. It's a perfect answer.

There was just one more person to complete the puzzle. The only problem is I have to come right out of my comfort zone for this hire.

SIX

ESHA

I check the address on my phone again. Yup, 631 East 1st Street. From the outside the place looks tired and neglected, but the large glass doors are open and there is a slow stream of contractors meandering in and out as I stand staring at what might be my next opportunity. The email inviting me to come along for an *interview* had come from a Sapphia Adamos. I have to admit the name of the place "Sapphy's Gym" didn't inspire me with confidence. My assumption is that Sapphia and Sapphy are one and the same.

Who names a gym after themselves?

From the outside and the name of the gym, I already make assumptions. It all reminds me of that gym out of Rocky - I can't quite get the name - Meaty Mike's or something similar. But the look, combined with the name, leaves me feeling less than enthusiastic.

It couldn't be more different from the place I went to see this morning, which was the newest branch of the *Elite Fitness* chain. The place was clean and spotless to the point of being sterile, much like the staff. They were 'courting' me to join their

team. I've taught yoga for eight years and training yoga instructors for the last four. Without being boastful, I am probably one
of the best known yogi in the city. If it hadn't been for the fact
my landlord was selling off my rent controlled studio, on the
other side of town, I wouldn't be having *these* conversations
with anyone.

A woman in her early thirties steps out onto the sidewalk,
followed by a muscly guy in a black T and a set of well-worn
cargo pants. The woman is tall, well when I say tall she is probably about five foot seven. Maybe? Compared to me, that's tall
but still shorter than the guy who has now slipped the pen from
behind his ear and is writing something on the back of his hand.
I watch as she points up to the brickwork above and to the right
of the door. Every muscle in her body is defined, with sculpted
curves elegantly running from one into another. Her brown
hair, which seems to be peppered with lighter streaks, most
likely from the sun given her skin's glow, is pulled up into a
ponytail revealing a powerful neck.

Is she Sapphy?

Rather than cross the street, I'm taking a moment to watch
her. Each movement, as she talks to the tall man, is animated
and oddly passionate. Arms move up and down, out to the side,
then thrown in the air in what seems to be frustration. By now
I've taken to leaning against the metal of the street sign which
declares this a residents' parking zone, such is the gentrification
of the area. If this is indeed Sapphy, she must have paid hand-
somely for that building because developers are snapping them
up at an alarming rate to build their four-story apartment
blocks. Something I am all too familiar with given my current
predicament.

As I stand and stare intently at their exchange, the woman
seems to sense my presence and looks over. I feel an odd urge to
wave back, but I don't. I suppress the impulse and avert my

eyes, acutely aware of my ogling. Looking directly at me, her arms drop to her side and she tilts her head. For a moment I think she is about to cross the street to speak to me. I shuffle my feet awkwardly but before she moves; the man says something and her attention returns to him and the task in hand. Another moment of energetic gesticulation follows, and then the pair head inside.

I check my watch. It's time to cross the street and meet the real Sapphia Adamos.

I feel slightly heartened when I walk through the doors into what I would imagine will be the reception area. A heavy, curved wooden reception desk sits to one side, still wrapped in layers of plastic and protective cardboard. Plastic runners have been taped to the floor, obviously to protect the newly laden wood. I walk deeper through a set of double open doors, emerging into a gym with a huge vaulted ceiling. There's stuff everywhere in varying states of unboxing, but right in the middle of the space, rising proudly up, is a huge boxing ring.

A woman approaches me with an enormous smile and dyed blonde hair, which is shaved at the sides and longer on top.

"Hi, are you Esha?" The woman tilts her head, raising her eyebrows in question.

"Yes, are you Sapphia?"

"No, I'm Abs. Sapphy is up in her office." She has eyes that match her smile and a soul that feels generous. "Did you find us okay?" she asks me. "Follow me. We haven't got the sign up yet. The contractors have been flat out getting in here sorted," Abs raises her arms indicating to the huge gym space, "so they haven't started outside yet."

I dutifully follow, wondering where they got these names from, I mean Sapphy and Abs...they sound like names from a bad lesbian comic strip.

Ahead of us is a black metal staircase. The thump of her

foot against the textured metal tread echoes as she runs up ahead of me.

"This is my office," she says as we pass the first door on the long gallery landing.

The offices have large glass fronts which give them a full view of the main gym. You can see how large the space is from this height and how much equipment they have. The ring stands in the center but it doesn't overwhelm the area; in fact, it looks fitting.

"And this is Sapphy's." Abs waves through the glass before opening the door.

The woman I saw earlier on the street is sitting behind the desk on the far side of the room. Abs throws the door open and steps inside, I follow.

"Sapphy meet Esha, Esha this is Sapphy," Abs says with a huge wide grin. "It was nice to meet you Esha." She nods and leaves me standing inside the office. The hollow thump of metal echoes as she runs down the stairs, two by two.

"Please come in and take a seat." Sapphy's voice is an octave or so deeper than I expected. It has a husky quality to it which is attractive.

As I walk towards the large white desk, she holds out her hand towards me. I take it and feel the warm touch of her skin. Up close, she is even more striking than at a distance. High cheekbones, deep brown eyes and full pink lips which turn up at the corners, all hold my attention. Her mouth is moving, and it isn't until she pulls her hand away that I realize that not only was I holding my breath, but I hadn't heard a word she said.

"Sorry, I—you have such a beautiful smile, I didn't hear you." My honesty seems to stun her momentarily, and then she laughs. A full, glorious, hearty laugh. Something fizzes in my stomach, and I'm pretty sure it isn't my avocado smoothie from breakfast.

"I'm not sure what to say to that, but thank you."

Her hair is down now. There are strands of almost a golden honey brown flecked against the darker mid brown and it falls in gentle waves on her olive-skinned shoulders.

Her smile has an infectious quality, and I grin back. "Do I call you Sapphy or Sapphia?" I ask, taking the seat opposite her.

"Call me Sapphy, please. If anyone calls me Sapphia, then I know I'm in trouble."

Oof that smile.

Crossing one leg underneath her, she lowers herself down onto her chair. It is one of those high-backed executive office numbers and sitting in her leggings and vest, I'm struck by the contrast between the two.

"Thanks for coming along and I hope you didn't mind me reaching out to you. When one of my old team said you were looking for a new opportunity, I thought a discussion might prove mutually beneficial."

"Okay." I pause wondering how forthright I should be at this stage. "I was curious when I got your email, but the word 'interview' concerned me. I'm not looking for a salaried position. I have a thriving business, which I need to relocate. I'm not handing over years of hard work for a few dollars an hour."

I breathe out deeply, only now appreciating how much tension I have been holding in my body, waiting to get that off my chest. I feel lighter.

"Yeah, sorry. That was an awful choice of words on my part. We've been so busy trying to organize everything, I must have gone on automatic pilot. I'm not looking to employ you, but we have a great opportunity for the right woman." She looks at me with a lopsided, apologetic smile. "I've done my research, checked you out—professionally, I mean."

Even her olive skin couldn't disguise the blush that rose up her neck before exploding in her cheeks.

"Look, why don't you tell me what you want from an opportunity and let's see if I can match it with what we have here. Deal?"

I nod. *Maybe there is more to this woman than meets the eye?*

I take my time explaining about my business, my reputation, my clientele and my current lease, which runs out in a matter of weeks. Sapphy listens intently, nodding as I speak. During that time she asks me why I don't just rent new premises. I answer her in the only way I know how; with complete honesty.

"I don't have the money to risk leasing out new premises. It isn't just the lease but the cost of fitting it out and then what if it is sold from underneath me, yet again. And I certainly don't have the money to buy. I'm not as young as you." As I say the last words, I can see a look of confusion cross her face.

"What age are you...? If you don't mind me asking?"

Perhaps it was my own directness that emboldened her, but I have nothing to hide.

"I'm forty-eight." My answer seems to shock her. Genuinely shock her. I've often been told I look younger, but it isn't something I ever think about.

"That's amazing...I mean, *you* look amazing for your age. Not that forty-eight is ancient or anything. It's not. It's just older than I thought and well you could be my—" falling over her words she halts, teetering on the edge of losing her balance irretrievably.

"My sister?" I offer with a smile.

Clearing her throat, she begins again. "What I am trying to say, badly, is that you don't look your age and that I find you very attractive. I mean—" Her eyes went wide above burning cheeks as she realized what she had just said, "—you are very attractive for your age, I mean, not that I don't find you attractive you understand. I just—shit, I am handling this incredibly badly and I apologize. I'm sorry." Sapphy shook her head and looked down at her desk.

"And you were doing so well." I laugh. She really is incredibly cute when she blushes, but I guess from the way she is cringing, cute isn't what she is *feeling* right now.

"I know, right?" As she covers her hands over her face, I can only laugh.

"Look, why don't you tell me about what you're building here. I'd love to know more about it and you have me at a disadvantage because...I didn't do my research before coming here. I like to keep an open mind and there are a few places I'm looking at today so..." I shrug, hoping the change of subject and putting her back in control again will help lower the intensity of red painted across her cheeks.

"Okay," she agrees with what seems like relief, and then she tells me all about Sapphy's.

Her eyes burn with passion, talking about her vision for the space, the business, but mainly for those who walk through the doors. The woman sitting in front of me is determined, focussed and committed to making this work. I can't help but be sucked in by her energy. By the time the conversation turns to how and where yoga will fit in, I am nodding in agreement.

"I know little about yoga, but from what I have read I think it would be a real benefit to everyone who trains here, and of course I'm not completely naïve. There will be some who come just for your classes. You'd have complete autonomy of what you'd teach, and when. Essentially, you rent the space and we provide you with all the facilities you need." We nod in unison. "You came highly recommended and I haven't approached anyone else. I wanted us to have a chance to speak first."

I'm flattered. I like her and yes, of course I'll sit down and make sure it all works on paper, but I get a good feeling about here; about Sapphy's; about Sapphy.

"I can show you around and introduce you to the trainers, too. If you have time?"

"I'd love you too."

As Sapphy leads me down the metal staircase, I can't help feel a little guilty about the slightly uncharitable thoughts I had (the place and their names) when I first arrived. Watching her in tight leggings and a tank top, I feel an odd stirring in my stomach. It's just an appropriate reaction to the business, I tell myself.

———

Between the gleaming new studio space with its sprung floor, a friendly team and reasonable rent, Sapphy's gym worked on paper for me, but more importantly it also worked in my gut. I always relied heavily on my intuition, gut, whatever you want to call it, and this time was no different. Sapphy insists I go away and think about my decision, but the reality is there's not a vast amount to think about. Moving my business here just feels right. The last piece of the puzzle, the clincher, is that my contract also offers me the use of one of the treatment rooms upstairs, so I can work both sides of my business from here, yoga and massage.

My phone pings again and another client confirms they have the new details for the class and books for next Tuesday. Although I have another two weeks on my current lease, I've agreed to move my classes across to coincide with the gym's opening week, which is only three days away.

Tonight is the "Grand Opening" a.k.a the big party to celebrate the launch. Sapphy is double and triple checking everything from the guest list (even though it's too late to add anyone now) to the caterers, as well as making sure everything is perfect. It is.

From her vision to managing the complete renovation, she isn't just talented; she is driven, determined, and tonight she is on a mission. We've become a little closer in the last couple of weeks. She impressed from the moment we met, but seeing her energy and passion day after day has left me slightly in awe. But I worry about her. She could easily burn herself out.

This is her night to take a break before the fun begins she told me with a laugh earlier. We evidently have very different ideas about what 'taking a break' looks like. At least she has agreed to let me practice a little yoga with her at lunchtimes and she is even contemplating one of my therapeutic massage sessions – both would be of benefit – *we'll definitely do it, next week*, she tells me.

"Esha, can you help us?" Logan shouts from behind two cases of champagne. "Abs is at the car and we've another ten boxes to bring in."

"Sure thing."

I rush out through reception, where two girls have set up a cloakroom in the front office, and then out onto the street. The tailgate is up and Abs is bent over with her head in the trunk. As I wait for Abs to pass me a box, Sapphy appears behind me and wraps her arms around my shoulders. Her warmth, her scent, her—my head swirls.

"I can't believe we've actually done it! I'm so excited. I hardly slept last night." She kisses my cheek and like a silly, irrational school girl, warm fuzziness builds inside me.

SEVEN

SAPPHY

My stomach is a fizz of excitement. I check my watch. 7:52 p.m. it declares in bold green digits. The invites said be here for 8 p.m. and we have a couple of dozen people here already. Abs is laughing with a few women as she tries to persuade them to get into the ring, and Logan is handing out glasses of champagne to a couple who've just arrived. I really hope tonight is a success.

I haven't eaten and I can feel the fizz go straight to my head. I'm not someone who drinks often, and even when I do, one glass is normally enough for me. I need to get food. Maura's insistence that we *spare no expense* means the table in front of me is laden with enough miniature food to feed half the city. I'm about to help myself to a tiny carved fruit kebab when I feel a hand on my shoulder.

"We were just saying how delicious everything looked." Esha's smile was open and warm, and I immediately find myself returning it. "I want to introduce you to Maggie. She is my oldest friend."

Maggie and I exchange nods and I fumble with my plate,

switching from one hand to the other, to allow me to offer my hand in greeting, but instead Maggie steps forward and hugs me. I hold my arms out slightly stunned but accept the friendly greeting.

"A friend of Esha's is a friend of mine and that earns you a hug," she declares, leaving me to mumble a surprised thank you. "And not just her oldest friend, but also her first client as well."

As Maggie pulls back, I look at her a little closer. Tall, elegant and lithe. She appears older than Esha. *I would think fifties, maybe?* But I thought Esha was in her early thirties, so I'm not placing too much faith in my estimations.

"It's good to meet you. Esha mentioned you've been helping her let everyone know about the changes." As I speak, I'm aware of Esha's soft gaze on my face. Over the last two weeks we've seen each other most days and already it feels like we've known each other for so much longer. Each morning I check my watch, wondering when she'll arrive. The other day I even made a point of being in the gym when I knew she was due to arrive, even though I had other things to do. There is something about her presence. It grounds me.

"Esha has been telling me all about you. It's so good to put a face to the name at last and you know Esha is right, you are very attractive."

"Maggie!" Esha blurts out, and for the first time I see what appears to be a blush on her dark skin.

Normally I am the one who ends up blushing as part of our encounters, so her response is reassuring. I give a slightly embarrassed giggle and cringe as I hear myself. Now, I too am blushing. Maggie just stands there, looking at us and beaming.

"I eh, I-I just thought I'd grab myself some food before we got busier. I don't want to drink on an empty stomach." I glance from the food up to Esha's face and for a moment our eyes lock.

I have the strangest sensation, as if someone has sucked all the air out of the room and time is still...and then with a loud commotion behind us, the moment is lost.

"What does a girl have to do to get a glass of champagne around here? Sapphy darling, you look spectacular. Is that the tux I sent you?" Maura's voice booms, echoing around the space as she literally shouts at me from across the gym. The click of her heels is growing louder as she approaches with purpose, and in my head I hear the theme from Jaws.

With two large air kisses, she greets me and places one possessive arm around my shoulders, smiling at Esha and Maggie. I blush again, but for entirely different reasons.

"Maura, this is Esha, she is our resident yogi, and this is her friend Maggie." I nod, smiling, and take in their slightly stunned expressions. Maura is a lot to take in. "And this is Maura," I say with no further explanation.

"Are you going to give me the guided tour?" Maura's barely even acknowledges Sapphy and Maggie and I blush a little at her rudeness. I'm used to her treating me like this but it irks me when she does it to other people, especially when it's such a good person like Esha.

"I'm sorry will you excuse me just for a short while?" I smile apologetically and allow myself to be dragged off by Maura. I show her the studios where Abs is with a crowd of women. Abs has them in the palm of her hand as they hang on her every word, but then she turns and her eyes fix on Maura with a glower.

"She needs to be more grateful," Maura mutters loudly as we leave.

She feigns interest as I show her the rest of the facilities, but Maura has never been one to hide her boredom. When we arrive back in the main gym, she focuses her attention on the black metal staircase.

"So will you run your *empire* from up there?"

Her emphasis on *empire* is typically condescending, but I choose to ignore it, as I always do.

"Maybe we should christen your office?" she says with a wink.

No. Not tonight. It's not that I'm not grateful for her help I am, but I just want tonight to be about—the gym. Thankfully, I don't get time to make an awkward excuse as her attention is drawn by the arrival of people who she invited along. I have no idea who they are, nor do I have any real desire to speak to them. On the few occasions I have been in the company of her *friends*, I've found it awkward. I'm the toy she discards when something shinier comes along.

"Hold that thought," she declares before sweeping off in her heels and tight black number to greet them.

I watch her greet them with air kisses and exclamations of "Darling, you look exquisite." They come from another world and one which certainly isn't mine. But that is okay. In my own way, in my little box which she places me, I am enough for Maura and there is an odd sort of security in that knowledge.

I'm still standing on my own, where she dumped me, when out of the corner of my eye I'm aware of someone watching me. I glance over, a little self-conscious. Esha tilts her head to the side and smiles. I blush.

———

My cheeks were aching midway through the evening. Schmoozing isn't something that comes naturally to me, and the event is proving to be more stressful than I expected. After the second hour, I hear myself repeating the same things over and over again; our mission, what we stand for, our values – all the buzzwords I'm supposed to say to sell the gym – and the message seems to resonate with guests. I can only hope their affirmations translate into memberships.

"I bet you wish you'd never worn heels," Abs says, then laughs as she approaches me during a rare moment of solitude.

I look down at my feet and nod. She wasn't wrong, but try as I might I couldn't find a pair of trainers I owned that looked good with a tux.

"What was Maura doing here earlier?" she asks with feigned innocence.

I shrug, staring at my feet, at these damned heels. It's one thing not to have mentioned who our generous benefactor is, but it's something else to lie.

"Sapphy, you didn't? Please tell me she isn't your investor?" Glancing up, I see her shake her head. A look of genuine concern is etches itself on her face. "Christ, is that why you avoid the subject every time I bring it up?"

"Abs, it isn't as bad as it seems. Honestly." I smile gently. I know most of Abs concern is because she cares about me. "It's a business deal and I pay it back in two years so the place will be mine and her stake in it will be gone. It's just two years."

"She treats you like shit, Sapphy." Her frown causes small vertical *what the fuck* lines to appear as her brows converge. "For the life of me, I don't get why you have anything to do with her."

Abs concern is always well placed, but Maura something we don't really talk about. It is the only bone of contention we ever have between us, and I can't bring myself to tell her the truth. It's one thing to know the answer, but it is another to say the words out loud.

Maura is what I deserve. She's safe because in the little box she puts me, I know I am enough.

EIGHT

I throw my backpack onto the floor and perch my coffee on the edge of the reception desk so my hands are free to punch in the alarm code. I have a grand total of forty-five seconds to input the right digits or the alarm goes into overdrive and boy is it loud. Logan didn't quite make the cut last Sunday, and she said the half the apartments on the opposite side of the street were peering out their windows. She was mortified.

I pick up a letter from the mat and head around to the back of the reception desk, flicking on the lights across the building from the central control panel. There is something nice about being in at this time of the morning when the whole place is filled with silence and anticipation. I do enjoy anticipation. I used to enjoy that first hour when I worked at Evolve as well, but here it's different. We've built this from scratch. This is my baby.

I hear whistling and realize it's coming from me. There have been a few times over the last few weeks since we opened for business where I've caught myself whistling or humming. It's not that I was grumpy before it's more that I'm filled with relief partly because we are now open and also that the team has gelled so well. Logan, Abs and I all knew each other, but we've never worked so closely before and never opened a business together. I expected there to be a few moments between us, but it's been plain sailing so far.

And then we added Esha into the mix. Her personality is very different to the three of us and she is way older, not that you'd know by looking at her, but she seems to bring a calm balance to our frenetic behaviour. There is just something about her energy that is different. I tried to say that to Abs, but she just laughed at me. 'Oh, her *energy?*' her teasing had echoed my words and when I blushed she laughed even more, announcing to anyone who was close enough to hear that I have a crush. By the time she was finished, I was scarlet with embarrassment from the top of my head to my knees.

I pick up my messages from the desk and sift through them as I sip my coffee. Logan's handwriting was even worse than mine, but the one on top simply says *Maura called–9.50 p.m. Call her back!* I'd crashed early last night and still hadn't gotten around to turning my phone back on. This was a new thing I was trying thanks to Esha. It had come up at a morning meeting we'd had to discuss adding extra yoga classes to the timetable. She had said I looked tired, and I'd admitted I was not a great sleeper. Try it, she told me, so I did. I turn my phone off half an hour before I go to bed, and then I don't turn it on until I arrive at work the next morning. The routine prepares your body for sleep. Weirdly it works, although for the first few nights I kept reaching for my phone only to be met with a black screen.

I powered up my phone as I went through the rest of the messages, but there was nothing of any significance. When the phone kicked into life, it announced I'd missed five calls from Maura and I had three voicemail notifications blinking at me. I sighed, then called voicemail, putting it on speaker so I could grab my backpack and coffee as I listened.

The first message asked for my presence at her place, telling me she'd be home in half an hour. 9.15 p.m. was the time stamp. I hadn't realized I'd turned my phone off so early. Her tone was a touch more terse in her second message. She had arrived home, and I wasn't waiting for her. The time stamp on that one told me she'd phoned the gym and no doubt bit Logan's head off straight after that call. That explains the exclamation mark on the message. The third and final message was at 11 p.m. and she was no longer making any attempt to hide just how pissed my absence was making her. *I expect to hear from you first thing tomorrow morning.*

Well, that silenced my whistling. Maura has always been demanding and when she shouts jump, I'm the first to admit I ask how high. Disappointing people is something I actively avoid, especially Maura. I've no doubt if I asked a therapist I'd be told that it has to do with my parents. That is one of the great things about having a punch bag as your therapist, it never states the damned obvious. I check the main door is locked and grab my stuff to dump it in my office. I've half an hour until we open and rather than worry about getting chewed up by Maura, I'd going to spend the time calming myself down.

Every punch I slam into the bag reverberates off the walls and ceiling. The harder I hit, the louder the echo and the more it soothes my soul. I check the big old station clock that sits high on the wall, I'm into my last minute before I have to stop and open the doors. With one huge right cross I slam my glove into the bag only to feel my shoulder kickback. I drop my right arm to my side and bend forward. I must have let out a yelp because I'm suddenly aware of somebody asking me if I'm okay. I jump in fright. My response is exaggerated and is way more marked than is either cool or appropriate. When I look up, I see Esha rushing over.

"Are you okay?"

"Yeah, I'm fine," I mumble in embarrassment. I never used to blush this much well not until I met Esha.

Shoving my gloves under my arms, I pull them off, first the right one, although the pulling action makes me wince and then the left so that I can try to knead my muscle.

"Stand up," Esha's hands are on my shoulder, her fingertips pressing their way over my shoulder and down towards my lats. "Do you mind if I feel under your tank?"

If she wasn't such a deft hand with soft tissue, I think her questions would have made my eyebrows shoot up, but I just nod. Her hand slides under my tank. Her fingers are warm. Her touch, gentle and firm at the same time.

"Lift your arm up to the side for me."

As she realizes I'm not wearing underwear, she hesitates. "It's okay. I don't mind if you don't but I am quite sweaty now. Not a great way to start your morning." I glance around behind me to where she is standing so I can gauge her reaction. I see the slightest smile. Rather than answer me, she let her fingers do the talking. When they hit the point she was looking for, I let out a small 'ouch' and pull back the smallest amount. But still she prods.

"You two need to get a room!" Abs shouts and again I jump, but this time out of awkwardness rather than fright. Esha's fingers glance over the soft skin at the side of my boob and for the briefest moment I forget about the pain, losing myself in her touch.

"Okay, we need to get it iced. Abs, are you okay if I steal my patient away for some treatment?" Esha grabs her bag and motions for me to follow.

"Yeah, I've got it covered down here. You two have fun." Abs winks as I pass her, and I return her cheek with a scowl.

This is the first time I've been in Esha's treatment room. There is a light sandalwood scent to the room, which isn't unpleasant. Sit on the edge of the bed, she says. I do. Esha opens a small fridge in the corner. The glass panel on the door offers an unobstructed view of bottles of water and ice packs.

Handing me a towel, she instructs me to hold it over my chest and remove my tank. I know what is coming next and I'm not looking forward to it.

"Hold the towel in place and lift your right arm up a little for me, please." She paused. "I know it's difficult but try to relax."

"Easy for you to—" I can't finish my sentence before the cold whips my breath away along with my words. I gasp as the acute pain of the cold against my skin takes effect.

"Don't forget to breathe," Esha teases, obviously enjoying my overly dramatic performance. "So do you always go at it with such force so early in the morning?"

"Only when I need to let off steam." Then a thought occurs to me and I feel compelled to ask, "How long were you watching me?"

Esha is standing behind me holding an ice pack on my right lat and her other hand is gently massaging my left shoulder. The contrast between the cold and the warmth is striking. I feel my shoulders begin to relax and drop.

"About ten minutes. There is something compelling about watching a powerful woman work out."

I'd be flattered if it wasn't for the fact that it was my lack of power that spawned the early morning workout. Now and then the irony of my situation hit me between the eyes with full force, and this was one of these moments. Here I was building a fitness business with a key mission of empowerment, and yet I run around trying to please Maura. No matter how much I try to convince myself that this *thing* suits my needs as much as hers, last night's trio of messages makes it impossible for even me to believe.

"So what made you want to blow off steam this morning?" Esha's tone is one of concern, her voice soft.

"Just some stuff with the person who invested in the gym. They can be quite demanding," I say, brushing off her question. She seems to sense it's something I don't want to talk about, so she lets it slide.

"You should try yoga as a way of releasing your frustration. It might be safer." Esha's hand continues to massage my left shoulder and I feel myself melt into her touch. There is something about her presence that grounds me.

"Thanks, but I'm not really somebody that joins classes." I sigh heavily, feeling more relaxed now. The muscle under the ice pack no longer feels any pain or cold. It's numb.

"So is it just the classes that put you off, or is it the idea of yoga itself?" Her question is direct and offers me nowhere to hide. It is one of the many things I like about her. She is open and transparent. There are no games, or manipulation, no hidden agenda's. I used to tell Abs that's what I liked about Maura, *it's honest and upfront about what 'it' is.* I think I believed it until I came across Esha. The reality is when you come across someone who really is honest and upfront, it blows the guise I've given Maura for all these years. *Still, we get what we deserve out of life, don't we?*

"Just the class," I mumble, enjoying her touch, perhaps a touch too much.

"So if I offered you a one-to-one session to help you relax then you'd say yes?"

"Mm," My mind is floating under Esha's touch and a one-to-one session sounds... "What? A one-to-one yoga session?"

"Yes. Just you and me." A small laugh follows. "Why, what did you think I meant? What other sort of private sessions do you have in mind?"

I blush, grateful this time she is standing behind my red cheeks.

———

"I'll leave you alone to get yourself comfortable. You can remove whatever clothing you feel comfortable with. You can leave your panties on. Then lie face down on the bed and cover yourself with a towel." Esha points to the towels at the end of the bed and leaves the room. It's been a few days since my first ice pack session and the inflammation on my lat has reduced enough for the next step, a massage.

I've been holding my shoulder a little tighter than usual, protecting it from any further injury, and that's just caused stiffness right across my shoulders on both sides and my back. I'd normally look forward to a good massage. It was always my treat after a match to reduce the muscle ache that was guaranteed to follow. But today I feel oddly nervous. I'm not sure why.

I lay face down on the bed. The towels beneath me are thick and soft. I place a larger towel over the middle of my back, pulling it down on either side, and when I feel comfortable, I stick my face into the hole. I'll have creases on my face for hours after this.

It had been a long few days and as expected Maura had chewed me out for not being available when the mood took her. I'd gone around the following night to appease her, and although I managed not to use my right shoulder, she seemed satisfied. I just feel drained.

The air in the room changes and I realize I was drifting off to sleep. I inhale deeply and open my eyes. I hear Esha move around the room in her quiet, understated way and my body pulls itself out of its pre-slumber. In a matter of minutes, her hands will be on my body. Slow rhythmic strokes await. Anticipation kicks in, my body tingles at the thought.

"I'm about to place my hands on your back, just breath deeply and relax," Esha's tone is soothing but rather than relax as she suggests the moment her hands make the first long, sweeping movements over my skin, I go into high alert. My body amplifies the volume of her touch until the air cracks with electricity. Slow repetitive movements excite and earth me at the same time. I feel confused.

I wonder, can she feel it too, or does this only exist in my head? In my body. I swear I've noticed a different energy between us in the last few days. I hear Abs laugh as I use the word energy yet again. It's not my word, it's Esha's but I seem to have adopted it. I like it. It describes perfectly what I feel between us. A spark. A positive charge of electricity.

We have moments, like yesterday, when her breath whispered against my neck as she leant over to study the schedules on my screen. This morning, as I held the door ajar for her and she squeezed past, brushing against me, her scent filling my senses. These *moments* between us seem to be more frequent, and they last longer.

Her fingers ease over my muscles, my arms fall to the side of the bed. Her touch is warm, causing my body to tingle. As she sweeps up my side, there is the merest glance against the side of my breast and my body fills with excitement. I swear I feel my clit twitch. I immediately chastise myself and force my body to relax. It doesn't work.

"You seem a little tense," she mumbles in a quiet tone, as if it is a passing thought that is meandering through her head.

Can she really not feel this? Does she want to touch me as much as want her too?

I've seen her look at me, her eyes moving slowly over my body. My body is firm, taut, and the one thing I gratefully inherited from my parents is deep olive skin. I'm used to people admiring me. I see their appreciation, but it is only skin deep. I dismiss these stares when they come, but the way Esha regards me is different. She looks deeper and that scares me.

Beyond what I have carefully sculpted, there is little of interest. What if she see's the chasm of emptiness inside me? What if she looks deep inside to that vault which makes everyone else *enough* and finds *nothing*? The idea panics me, but still the thought of her never looking again fills me with even more dread. I need her to keep seeing me.

Her warm hands glide over my skin, her pressure increasing now, and I moan into the hole where my face is planted. *Please don't stop.*

"I'm just going to pull down the towel a little and adjust your panties. Okay?"

I manage a grunt, all the while wishing I had removed *all* my clothing. I feel her tug the elastic and the cotton rubs against my skin. Her hands massage the top of my butt cheeks and a jolt of exhilaration shoots through me before fizzing wildly in my core. My body moves unconsciously, my legs parting almost imperceptibly before I can attempt to stop it happening. I roll my eyes behind closed lids. My body wants what my body wants and right now I am at its mercy. *Let your hands slide downwards, please. Let your fingers—*

"Okay, we are about done here," her words are gentle but my body screams, *No, I need more. So much more.* Her weight is placed evenly over my back as though she is trying to push any last tension out of my body. If only she knew the turmoil I feel inside.

Warmth comes from the towel she places over me. "Lie still

for a few moments and then when you are ready, take your time and get dressed. I'll come back in a few minutes."

The door closes. I moan gently into the hole and stare at the light oak floor. A chuckle erupts from my chest. I am ridiculous. Horny as fuck and ridiculous. Here I am, hot and bothered, and Esha has been nothing but professional. Of course she doesn't feel the same *energy*.

It takes an enormous effort to summon the power I need to push myself up and swing my legs over the side of the bed. I sit for a moment, allowing myself to adjust to this new vertical position. A bottle of water sits at the side, ready for me, and I grab it, screwing off the cap to take a large gulp. I am so thirsty.

I consider my clothes carefully before sliding off the edge of the bed. I adjust my cotton panties and grab my leggings, hauling them up the length of my legs and shaking my bum into position. I place my sports bra and vest in front of me. I don't always wear a sports bra unless I know I'm coming to workout but today I felt I should, even if it is just out of modesty. There are so many things I am do with an awareness of Esha. Wearing a sports bra, checking the schedule to see when she'll arrive, and spending an inordinate amount of time walking along the corridor in front of the yoga studio.

These things happen despite me. Despite the fact I know nothing good will ever come of it. Esha is a woman who has depth. I do not.

A light knock fills the room and Esha walks in. My sports bra and tank still lie on the bed in front of me. Lost in thought, time has moved faster than I have.

"Oh, I'm sorry I'll—," she stutters.

"No, it's fine. Come in. I'm fairly sure you've seen it all before." I smile at my assumption. Does she often look at semi-naked women? Is she even interested in women? But then I see her look at my breasts. Her eyes linger that moment too long and then her tongue...her tongue presses against her bottom lip before she bites down, sucking the plumpness into her mouth. *Oh, she likes women all right, or at least she likes me.*

Sapphy get a hold of yourself. Even if she does *like* you, this is going nowhere.

NINE
ESHA

I checked the schedule yesterday. Abs is covering the reception for the last hour tonight. I want—I need to talk to her, but I don't want to make a big deal out of this. I need it to be casual, as if I'm mentioning random thoughts that are floating through my head at that moment. Being contrived is something I'm exceedingly bad at. As Maggie always tells me, it's a good thing I never became a defense lawyer.

I push through the double doors and I see Abs sitting behind the large wooden desk. The foyer is empty. The entire gym is quiet, except for a couple of women sparring in the far corner. I take a deep breath and pull my rucksack higher onto my shoulder. A flutter of nervousness rises in my tummy.

"Hi Abs," I make my voice as casual as I can.

Her head turns from the screen when she hears my voice. "Oh, hi Esha. That you finished?"

"Yeah, that was a long one today." I've practiced what I'm going to ask a thousand times in my head. *So, you and Sapphy? You've been like friends forever, haven't you?* In my head it sounds free and easy, but now standing in front of Abs I falter. She'll see right through me, I'm sure of it.

"You okay?" She tilts her head and looks at me with curiosity.

"Eh, yeah, I mean—" This is so much harder than it ever was in my imagination. I'm a 48-year-old woman for christ sakes. I sigh, defeated by my sheer lack of cunning. I'd never make a spy, that's for sure. Fuck it. I only have one mode in which I'm effective, and that's just honest. "I wanted to ask you about Sapphy." I shrug and roll my eyes as I watch a huge smile break out across Abs face.

"I knew it." Her hand slaps the desk in front of her and her eyes look triumphant. "I damn well knew there was something going on between you two."

"No." I have to correct her. "There's nothing going on between us," I explain, and I watch her smile evaporate. "I mean, not yet." I cringe hearing my own words. This is not how this conversation is meant to go.

"Oh, yeah, but you want there to be something?" Abs cocks her head, waiting on my response.

I sigh and smile. I need to just come out with this. Abs is easy to talk to, and I curse myself for trying to be clever.

"At the risk of sounding like a hormonally challenged teenager, yes I would. Very much." I nod more to myself than to Abs as consider my words. "We've become close over the last couple of months and I'm thinking about asking her to dinner, it's just..." I hesitate. "I don't want to make things awkward here and if there was a reason she might say 'no' then maybe it's better I just don't ask the question."

"She'd be off her head to say no to you." Abs laughs. She is incredibly sweet.

"Thanks for the vote of confidence. You seem to be more sure of the outcome than I do," I admit with a shrug. "I'm not the most accomplished flirt but I've been trying to—I don't know, give off the right signals? Only, either I am even worse flirt than I thought, or she just isn't interested and I'm not sure which it is."

Abs nods her head slowly. She seems to understand.

"I'm a little out of practice." I smile at Abs as again she nods slowly but says nothing, so I keep rambling. "I thought I'd ask you because, well, you are her closest friend and I thought maybe she might have said something." My voice rises, as do my eyebrows, in question.

"I think the two of you would be great together." She pauses and I stop myself from filling the silence. "Sapphy doesn't really do relationships. Hasn't for years. Not since Paula and that was like waaay back." Abs looks up to the corner of the room as if she is working her way through her mental filing system. "Yup, always single."

My heart slumps down into my stomach. I really thought there was something there, a connection.

"She's never seen anyone?" I ask as it seems strange to me that someone like Sapphy is single, never mind *always single*.

"No, not since Paula and that was back in college. She's not like a nun or anything. She see's people, you know, casually."

"Okay." I lift my backpack, which I laid at my feet when we started talking. "I suppose that answers my question, I'm glad I asked now that could have made things a little awkward."

"That doesn't mean she'll never see anyone. Right?" Abs offers me a look of encouragement. "Esha, I've never seen her act the way she does around you, with anyone else. It's weird, but kinda sweet." Abs smiles. "Just ask her. She might surprise us."

Maybe there is a chance. Maybe I'm not going crazy and there is a spark between us. I know there's lust, from my part anyway. She makes my body feel...alive, but there is something more. Something different. I've not felt this way in years about anyone. I've not avoided relationships in the way Abs seems to suggest Sapphy does, I just haven't found anyone that lights the spark. Until now.

"I might ask, we'll see. I'll think about it." I purse my lips together into a resigned smile. It's nice to hear that Abs can see *something* between us, but I'm no further forward. In fact, I might be a little farther away than I was before.

"So you and that woman you came to the opening party with? I thought you two were..." Abs stops as she hears my laughter.

"What, Maggie? Me and Maggie? God, no. I mean, we did years ago." I feel the need to explain. "She was a lawyer in a firm where interned when I was at college. It was pretty intense for a while, but no, not now. We're just great friends." I chuckle at the thought of Maggie's face if she heard what Abs was saying. "I'm about twenty years too old for Maggie." I watch as Abs eyebrows raise in surprise. "You'd stand much more a chance with Maggie than I would." I laugh, watching the perfect 'o' her mouth is forming.

I throw my backpack over my shoulder and head for the door. I need to give this some thought.

TEN

SAPPHY

Abs proudly hands me the membership report for the end of our first quarter, and it has exceeded all expectations.

"We're 60% up on what we projected on the uptake for annual gym-only memberships and all-in memberships are even better. We're 85% over target." Abs grins proudly.

Given how good Abs is with people, giving her responsibility for membership and staff was logical and she is excelling in her new role. Her enthusiasm never fails to turn interest into memberships as more and more people sign up. One of the local newspapers contacted us for a lifestyle piece in their weekend supplement, telling us the gym was the hottest commodity in town for women's fitness. I can't even describe how good but equally surreal it was to hear.

"Logan's Krav Maga classes are almost fully booked. There are two places left and I've got two women coming in this afternoon that might snap them up. Beth Brownley?" Abs says the name as if it is supposed to mean something to me, but I just shake my head. "She said we came highly recommended. I wasn't sure if it was an old *Evolve* customer?" Abs nods as I shrug absently and move on. "And Esha is doing a storm. She's had full classes every day, even the additional four classes she added are at capacity."

"You're doing great, Abs. I knew you would, and if we keep going at this rate, who knows we might pay Maura back sooner."

I smile, knowing that Abs would like nothing better than to have Maura out of the equation altogether. The reality is, the invoices for the renovation are still coming in and it is going to take a minor miracle to pay back Maura within the two-year timescale. A gentle knock causes us both to turn towards the door. Esha is standing signaling she could come back later, but I waved her in.

"Come in and grab a seat. Abs was just telling me how busy you are. Not that I hadn't noticed." My words make Esha smile; an easy, gentle smile that shines from her eyes. I melt.

Abs looks from Esha to me. "I'll leave that with you," she says, handing over the rest of the report. "I've got to cover reception over lunch." Shooting me a wink, she leaves us alone.

We, Esha and I, have been spending more time together. It is all an attempt to help me unwind. This has become our daily routine, a part of the day I look forward to. As the morning progresses, I check my watch far more often than I should, counting down to when I'll see her. Everything inside me screams I should leave things be and not rock our happy little boat by telling her how I feel. Besides, what would be the point, it would never go anywhere. But still I can't seem to stay away.

Esha pushes the chair to the side. She grabs two mats from behind the door and rolls them out, side by side.

"Come here, onto your mat. We'll start with a few warming stretches. Assume your usual position," she says with a rise of a single eyebrow and I do as I'm told.

I sit on the center of the mat, legs crossed, facing Esha. I find my flexibility increasing with each session, and sitting in this position is becoming more natural. I look directly into her eyes as she tells me to drop my shoulders and roll them back. I follow her lead. I'd never been conscious of how much tension I hold in my body, but it's amazing just how much distance I can now get between my shoulders and my ears when someone as beautiful as Esha tells me to relax.

"Now we're going to focus on the breathing. Close your eyes and rest your hands on your knees."

"The view is much better when my eyes are open," I tease.

"Your breathing," Esha says, closing her eyes. "Inhale deeply through your nose..."

I close my eyes and listen to her voice, following her every word. She is used to my nervous flirting now and doesn't rise to it. When a flirtatious comment bursts out, she gazes at me and I feel the hairs on the back of my neck stand to attention. More and more I want to fall into the deep warmth of her eyes. But for now, they are closed.

"And as you exhale, open your eyes and slowly raise your arms up, reach to the ceiling. One at a time reach to the ceiling, lengthening through your waist..."

We start each session like this and I know in a moment she'll have me twist my body and then move onto a whole cat, cow thing followed by warrior poses. Each session she changes it up a gear and adds new moves. Despite myself, I'm really enjoying it. I'll never remember all the names she gives each move, but that doesn't matter, the fact is I am getting stronger, more flexible. When my stance isn't quite right, I feel hands on my body, lifting my hips or straightening my shoulders. A jolt of energy fizzes through me and I have to work hard to swallow it down.

By the end of the session, I feel calmer, better. A twinge in my shoulder causes me to move my shoulder awkwardly when I roll the mat. I glance over and see Esha watch me.

"It's nothing. It's been way better since you treated it," I assure her. "But if you feel I need more work..." I let my words hang, ever hopeful.

"So you want my magic fingers then." Esha ripples her long thin fingers in such a way that I catch myself holding my breath. I can't take my eyes off them.

I want your fingers and you, more than you know.

"I-I, I don't want to take up too much of your time. That wouldn't be fair," I stutter, shocked by own—arousal. Yup, as I move from one foot to the other, I can confirm that is exactly what I'm feeling.

"You wouldn't be. Besides, we need to remedy it if I'm ever going to get you to Bakasana." Esha laughed and then seeing my blank expression she explains. "The crow pose, like this."

Esha crouches on the floor and then placing her weight through her shoulders, she lifts the rest of her body off the ground.

"Wow. Once you have me doing that, I will definitely owe you dinner." I laugh, unable to hide just how impressed I am.

Esha lowers herself back down with a giggle. "I was hoping I might offer you dinner before then?" Her gaze never leaves my eyes while she waits for my response.

My stunned silence fills the room. I want to say yes, please. Yes, I'd love that. But I say nothing. My mind is overthinking and I know it.

Is she asking me on a date? No, she is asking me as a friend. But if it is a date, then it's complicated. We work together. And Maura.

As if sensing my inner turmoil, Esha reaches out and places a hand on my arm. Something inside fizzes again. "I just want to say thank you. You've been very kind. And..." she hesitates.

Then with a blinding smile, she continues, "I'd like to get to know you better, Sapphy."

My heart did a backflip and before I could stop myself I hear myself say, "Yes, I'd like that a lot."

"Good. I'll send you my address. How does Saturday sound? Say eight?" I nod, probably with too much eagerness. "Come hungry, I enjoy cooking."

"Can I bring anything? With me...to dinner?"

"Just bring yourself." She reaches up and kisses me lightly on the cheek.

By the time I come back down to earth, Esha's footsteps are a mere echo on the metal staircase.

Did that really just happen? Have I agreed to a date? A mixture of excitement and nervousness bubbles through my head.

Saturday is three days away, and right now that feels like forever.

ELEVEN

"I'll see you later." Esha winks as she walks past Abs and I, leaving for the day. I blush as I feel Abs's eyes on me.

"Something you want to share?" she enquires with a certain amount of amusement.

"It's nothing. We're having dinner tonight. She wants to say thank you is all."

Abs lets out a chuckle.

"What?"

"Yeah, that's why she was asking me earlier this week if you were seeing anyone." She shakes her head. "See, that is why you've spent so much of your time being single. You can't see what is right in front of your face."

"You don't even know if she likes women. She was probably just making conversation." As I say the words, I really hope it isn't true.

"Man, you're completely blind, Sapphy. She is crazy about you, she's been flirting like mad and you can't see it. You just keep doing that crazy nervous flirting thing you do with every-one." I watch as Abs shakes her head again. "And for the record, that woman loves women. Remember Maggie that was here with her on opening night?" I nod in answer to her question. "Yeah, well, they are friends now but..."

"How do you know these things?" I'm incredulous.

"I listen, so people tell me stuff. You should try it sometime." She gives me a cheeky grin. "Now, you better get ready for your date. You've got a shitload of work to do."

―――

I've not seen Maura for weeks now. She bailed on me on to head to another *friend's* party on opening night, and since then I've only been summoned to *report in*, once. That's typical Maura. She becomes bored, or I bore her. I'm never sure which, but it's beside the point. She gets a better offer and her attentions go elsewhere.

Dipping in and out of people's lives is what she does. It had happened too often for me to take offense. If anything, her absence is something I'm enjoying. I feel guilty acknowledging my relief given everything that surrounds me is down to her generosity. I will have to call her to update her with the last quarters figures, but I don't want to think about that, or her, not tonight.

The clock on my dash tells me I'm twelve minutes late. I've sent a text to let Esha know. I don't want her to think that I'm not coming, or for my tardiness to spoil her cooking efforts. Google maps tells me the old colonial style building coming up on the right, with its blue hued wooden paneling, is the address I'm after. There is a small yard in front which is covered in an array of pots full of blossoming flowers.

Locking the car with a bottle of red wine in hand, I inhale deeply and head to her door. Something fizzes inside me, and I have no idea if it's excitement or nerves. Maybe it is a combination of both. What I do know, is that this is different. Different to anything I've felt before and for the first time it feels scary.

Sapphy, for God's sake, pull yourself together. Stop reading too much into this. You are friends. Nothing more. You can do this.

I used to talk to myself before a fight to put my head into the right space, but the difference between then and now is that I knew what I was doing in the ring. I'd trained for it. This— tonight, well, this is out my comfort zone.

After Paula left for the west coast, I couldn't eat or train, and I barely got out of bed for the first couple of weeks. I thought my life was over. It's probably why I always went back to Maura. It was easy and guaranteed, so I never end up feeling that level of pain again.

What the hell am I doing now? With every step I take, panic inside me is screaming, *turn back. Turn around and head back to the car. Now.* But my feet keep moving forward. I'm aware of everything. The crunch of the gravel under my sneakers as I walk up her path, the way the warm evening air brushes against my cheeks. It's as if my nerves have increased the volume. But still I keep moving forward.

Last chance. This is your last chance to turn around. My chest tightens.

The metal of the knocker is cold against my hand as I rap it sharply, announcing my arrival, and my stomach flips as I hear footsteps approach the door. I swallow hard.

As the door opens, warm light floods the porch. An aroma of spices wafts around me. My senses tingle. Esha stands in front of me like a mirage. Her long dark hair is draped over the shoulders of a deep red cotton shirt. She is stunning. Her smile is wide and her mouth is moving, but words don't register: all I can hear is the sound of great sheets of ice melt from my heart. Suddenly running *away* is the last thing I want to do.

It is the feel of a grip on my arm that brings me back into the moment.

"Come in and let me take your jacket."

I return her smile, stepping through the door. Immediately, it feels like coming home.

———

"Honestly, I can't eat another thing." I raise my hands in surrender. "This is some of the best food I've ever eaten. You're a talented cook. I promise to never cook for you because I would be such a disappointment." I laugh but there is no joke in what I'm saying. "Everything I cook comes with a ping at the end. But you? This? Just incredible."

"You impress too easily, but with praise like that I'd be happy to cook for you again." Esha's eyes gleam with pride.

"I will hold you to that, in fact I might just move in, your cooking is so good." I blush almost immediately as I see her eyebrows rise and I realize what I have just said. I stumble to recover. "So are you self taught? Or did someone teach you?"

Esha looks away, her smile fading.

What have I said?

"You are very kind," Esha says, but doesn't look up to meet my eye. "My grandmother taught me to cook when I was small. It's a long story and I'm sure you don't want to hear it." Her hand dismisses the thought I would be interested.

"Tell me. I'd love to listen if you want to share?" I smile to encourage her to continue and much to my relief, she does.

"My father's family came from Madhapar in India, but he moved here to study and then never went back. He was the only son, and when my grandfather died, my dadi came over to live with me and my mom and dad." Esha shrugs but I nod for her to keep going. "She didn't speak any English, and I think she found it all a little scary. My mom and dad were out at work a lot, my dad taught mathematics at the college, and my mom worked in the registration office so often that it was just dadi and me. I was lucky. She made me feel very loved."

When Esha looks up, she smiles, but her eyes are sad and wet. Instinctively, I move round to sit by her, taking her hand in mine.

"I'm sorry. I didn't mean to upset you," I say, rubbing my thumb over the smooth skin on the back of her hand. "Your dadi must have been an amazing teacher—and a wise woman to have loved you."

Her face offers me such a beautiful smile. I'm overcome with a need to place my lips against hers. But I don't.

"You would have loved her, Sapphy. Her heart was so big. So full of love." She pauses as I wipe away a single tear from her cheek. "It's hard to believe my father was born of her."

"We don't have to talk about this if you don't want to." I don't know what she means but I can see her pain. My heart aches for her.

"I know," she whispers, squeezing my hand. "Talking about my family can sometimes be hard, but to understand a person, you must understand what has shaped them. For me, it was the extremes of family. My dadi whose love was so pure and kind, and then my father who held expectations in his heart where there should have been love."

Another tear rolled down her cheek. I moved a little closer, wrapping both my hands around hers.

"Sometimes disappointing the ones you love is painful. I didn't choose to disappoint them I was just born that way. I was every inch the dutiful daughter, I studied hard, I gained my degree in law and I-I even married the man my father chose for me." A long sigh escaped, and she seemed to deflate. "But when I became pregnant, it was too much. I had to get out. I knew none of it was right. I was living a lie. They trapped me in somebody else's life. My mom begged my dad to allow me to return home, but he said no, forbidding my mom and dadi from seeing me. *Your place is with your husband*, he told me. But I knew that was wrong. I didn't know where my place in the world was, but it wasn't with the man I married. I miscarried not long after I walked out of the home we shared." I wiped away her tear with my thumb. I had no words to offer her, no wisdom to impart. I was just there. "My father said losing the baby was judgment of my behavior."

We sat in silence for several moments, just holding each other's hands, holding the pain between us.

"Esha, I'm so sorry you had to deal with that. Was it because you—"

"Loved women?" Esha's eyes glistened as she looked at me. "In part, I suppose it was, but my mom always said that it might not have been as bad if I had just refused to marry. I could have been excused or hidden in such a way that it didn't bring shame to the family, but marrying and then leaving my husband, losing our child...the shame which that brought on our family. That is what he could never forgive. It all happened so long ago. A lifetime ago...twenty-four years ago, but still it can make me cry."

Wiping a tear away, she smiled.

"You must think I'm awful. I invite you here and then break down in front of you. All because you complimented my Kadhi."

I lean back against the sofa and pull her into me, wrapping my arms around her. All I want to do is keep her safe.

"What about you? Are you close to your family?" she asks, her warm breath caressing my collarbone as she snuggles in.

"No. We didn't see eye to eye on lots of things, but I was never the dutiful daughter. I just rebelled. There were lots of arguments. I was a headstrong, defiant teenager." I grimace thinking about it.

"I can imagine that. You are a force of nature, Sapphy. A pure force of nature." She places her hand on my cheek. I tilt my head to feel her fingers move against my skin. I haven't sat like this, so closely wrapped in emotion with anyone since...Paula.

"And when I found a girlfriend, the sky fell in."

"Was that an act of rebellion?" Her question takes me by surprise, but the answer is easy.

"No, that was love." My answer is honest and a feel of rush of emotion wash over me. Emotion that I had been pushing down for years. I swallow hard, feeling a little choked, and I take a moment to gather myself before speaking again. I don't know whether Esha senses the change in me, but she pulls me a little tighter.

"They didn't like the didn't like the fact I love women and they certainly didn't like Paula, the girl I loved. In the end, there wasn't much they did like about me. The last time I saw them was at my youngest brother's wedding. He insisted on inviting me. I went because I love him but it wasn't—" I wasn't sure what the right word was. It seemed petty compared to what Esha had experienced. "It wasn't fun."

Wrapped in intimacy, we held each other in silence, lost to a world of thought about our own lives and that of the others; what might have been, and now what might be?

"Will you stay tonight?" Esha whispered.

I didn't answer with words but tightened my arms around her, giving a gentle, affirmative squeeze. I wasn't going anywhere.

———

There is no ripping off of clothes as we enter the bedroom, no mauling or groping. Instead, every movement is tender. I feel my stomach flutter with nerves as we undress one another. This matters to me. The touch of Esha's sweet, smooth skin against my own is overwhelming. A surge of emotion rises within me as we stand naked in each other's arms, with only the muted moonlight illuminating the room.

"Maybe we should go under the comforter?" she suggests with a shiver. The days are more mellow as we head into summer, but nights still hold a chill and all I want between us is warmth. I nod silently, following her as our limbs tangle together. Every kiss she places on my lips is filled with care. There is a tenderness in her eyes I want to sink into, to lose myself to.

Our hands run slowly over each other bodies, exploring curves and dips. I'm aware of everything. The sound of her quiet breath, the coolness of the sheets beneath us, the heat of her skin next to mine. I am consumed by her.

As we lie together, our noses touching, I lift her leg over mine, drawing us closer still. My glides down between us, tickled by short trimmed hair, until I feel the wetness of her desire for me. For us.

"Is this okay?" I whisper. The importance of making sure she is safe, matters.

"Yes." She places her lips against mine and gently rocks into my hand. As I slide over her swollen nub, and she lets out the smallest gasp. I kiss her gently, then slide one finger deep inside and then two. We move in perfect rhythm until I lose the sensation of where my body ends and hers begins. We mold into one.

Her moans increase, as does the tempo of my fingers, pressing against her G-spot. Our kisses are urgent, needy, as if we need every part of us to be forever connected. In and out,

out and in, over and over again. Rocking together, heat building heat within us until she clamps tight against my fingers, as her orgasm rushes over us.

I ease my fingers out, eliciting a shudder from her unwound body and I hold her tightly, relishing this moment, this feeling. One I thought I'd never feel again.

TWELVE

I awake to the sound of singing and the sweet smell of pancakes wafting through the house. Something feels so very right as I lay cocooned between the thick cotton sheets, which still hold the warmth of our bodies. We fell asleep holding each other and deep inside me, something changed. I don't know what it is or how to describe. All I know is the world just makes a bit more sense.

Even sitting at my desk now, hours later with the sound of metal plates clanging, there is a warm, round ball of—*something* within me. Esha that has awoken a change in me, and it feels good. Too good to lose.

"Well, don't you look like the cat that got the cream," Abs exclaims as she wanders into the room and plants herself on the chair opposite. "Did someone get lucky last night?"

My usual retort to Abs would be to tease her back, perhaps even suggesting that she was jealous, but not today. I feel myself blush.

"It's not like that," I shoot back, suddenly aware of the slight irritation in my tone.

"I'm just teasing." Abs considers me for a moment, then fills with a puzzled concern. "So did it go okay?"

"Yes." My voice is soft and I find myself smiling again as I have done since leaving Esha's house. "Abs, she is—" My eyes widen and my chest lifts as if I'm searching the skies for the perfect word, but there isn't one that is *enough* to describe what she is to me. What I feel.

Abs says nothing. Instead, she holds me steady in her gaze. Unblinking.

"I don't know how to describe it, to describe her, to describe how she makes me feel. I'm somewhere between deliriously happy and outright terrified. I'm all over the place." As I speak, I watch the corners of Abs's mouth turn up, until she sits in front of me in a full-blown grin.

"Shit, you've got it bad!" She laughs. "Well, damn, this is something I thought I'd never see. Sapphy is in love."

"I'm not in love. Don't be ridiculous. We've had like one date." I know I've bitten back too hard, but I'm so confused.

"Is this Sapphy's rules of love number one? You can't feel love until you've what had fifty bone fide dates? Can you even hear yourself?" She shakes her head, but she is still smiling. "Have you thought about anything else since you got here?"

"No," I admit sheepishly.

"Have you eaten anything since you left her...what was it last night? Or this morning?"

"It was this morning and no, but she made me pancakes for breakfast, so—"

"If I said she has just walked in downstairs and—"

I stand at my desk, cutting her off before she finishes. "She hasn't got a class today, it's her day off."

"Will you sit down? I'm teasing. But look at yourself. Sapphy, you might not be ready to admit it to yourself, but you've got it bad. Whatever you want to call 'it'." Her grin is so wide it forms a huge dividing line across her face. "Trust me, if anyone knows about complicated feelings and that first rush of love, well it might just be me."

I sit back down. I'm not ready to take on board everything Abs is saying, so I change the subject. "How is Hayley? She hasn't been in much?"

"She's good. Gracie's physio appointments take up her days off, so there isn't much time for the gym, but she'll get back to it. They both will. Which reminds me, can I get Thursday off to take Gracie? It's at 9:00 and Hayley will have just finished a night shift, so I said I'd take her. You don't mind, do you?"

I tell her I'll cover; she declares I'm the best and almost skips out the office. So that is what love does for you. Any minute now I'll break into skipping. The thought amuses me and I giggle quietly as I pick up my phone, which is vibrating to gain my attention.

The name on the screen kills my smile.

Maura.

My thumb hovers over the green and red phone icons. If I swipe the red icon, I allow myself to enjoy this feeling inside for that much longer. If I swipe the green phone, then I deal with the issues at hand.

I hit green.

"Well, you took your sweet time. I was beginning to think you'd changed your number." There was a caustic edge to her voice. Maybe she is annoyed I didn't answer on the first ring. Maybe that's her natural tone but I just hadn't noticed it before.

"Hi Maura, it's been a while."

"Have you missed me?" she says playfully.

I want to say no. It is an honest answer, but something tells me that wouldn't be a wise move.

"Mmm." Is as much as I can muster and even that took more effort than I would have liked.

"I'm at a loose end tonight, so I thought it might be nice to combine a bit of business and pleasure? You can bring over the reports and we might find something to entertain ourselves with when you're here?"

I marvel at how she can make it sound like I have a choice. But I do, and I choose not to.

"I can't." I'm blunt to the point of being almost rude. "I have other plans tonight," I say, trying to soften the message a little.

There's silence. Followed by more silence. Before, I'd have panicked at the sheer sound of nothing, and then yielded to its power with a stream of placations. But not today. Each of us remains locked in position like two chess players. One of us will have to give way; it won't be me.

"Be at my office tomorrow at ten sharp. I want last quarters report and the next six months projected costs and sales."

"Maura, it's Sunday afternoon, I've got last quarters report but I don't have the projections."

"I've told you what I want."

"Telling me now that you want six months' projections for tomorrow isn't fair, and you know it." I can feel irritation burn my cheeks.

"I'm not asking more of you than I do any of our other investments and Sapphy, don't bring the attitude. You are much more attractive when you are compliant."

Anger flushes through me, but before I can unclench my jaw and spit back a reply, the line goes dead.

———

I'm still sitting at my desk wading through figures when Esha calls. The gym is in darkness. Yvonne, our receptionist, locked up half an hour ago, dropping the keys in the lockbox. I take the call, knowing there is nothing I want more than to finish here and drive out to her place. But I can't.

The lightness in her voice is replaced with concern as soon as she realizes I'm still at the gym. Trying to explain why I can't say no to Maura's demand is tough, and that's without trying to explain the other part of the deal I'd agreed to get this place.

I can hear the disappointment in her voice and I apologize. If there had been any other way, I would explain, but I needed to get these figures done for tomorrow. I sigh as I come off the call. It fills the room, making the air that much heavier.

I've two months projections completed when I hear the double door downstairs swing open. The place is still in darkness. I sit completely still. Listening. Who the hell is here? My eyes dart around the room looking for something heavy, something I can use to defend myself.

Silently pushing my chair back, I get up and walk towards the door. Then I hear it. Footsteps on metal. They are coming up the steps. They are heading towards my office, towards me. The office lights. They have seen the light in the office. The darkness of the gym means they can see me, but I can't see them.

Fuck, why didn't I think of this when I was designing the place?

The sound of my heart crashing against the inside of my chest is deafening and I daren't breathe. I'm standing against the office wall directly behind the glass door. The shadow of an arm reaches out and pushes open the door and I instinctively grab the first thing that comes to hand and swing it towards the figure coming towards me.

"Ouch," Esha cries as the yoga mat bounces off her head. "What the—Sapphy, what are you doing?"

A mixture of adrenaline and relief erupts from me in a high-pitched giggle. "I'm sorry, I didn't know it was you. I thought someone...(more giggles) I thought someone had broken in."

"And you chose a yoga mat to defend yourself?" she says incredulously.

"I know." I couldn't do anything but laugh.

"Aren't you meant to be like some sort of martial arts big shot, with trophies belt and yet your weapon of choice is a yoga mat?" Esha couldn't help but join me in laughter as she nursed her right ear. "I'm just thankful I'm not teaching you baseball."

"Why are you here, anyway?"

"I came to help. Two heads are better and faster than one and you sounded a little stressed, so here I am. Put me to work, boss," Flashing a wide smile, she held open her arms and I grab her, hugging and twirling her around the office. "Well, that's a better hello than the last one."

Maybe Abs is right.

THIRTEEN

I pull into the parking lot of Maura's office building with two minutes to spare. I slept through the alarm, which is hardly surprising given it was a little after three this morning by the time Esha and I finished the projections. I'd given Esha a ride home, but rather than stay, I headed back to my condo. That way I figured I'd have more time in the morning and I wouldn't need to run around like crazy. Pulling on my jacket over my gym gear as I got out of the car, I mused about how well that plan had worked out for me.

I smile sweetly at the receptionist and I take a moment to realize it is a new receptionist—she's still blonde, pale pink lips, hair pulled up in a bun but this is a younger model. Only Maura could have a type when it came to receptionists.

"Miss Adamos, for Miss Hearst. I have a 10 am with her."

The girl checks the diary app, running her finger down the screen. "Ah, yes. Miss Hearst is running late. She has asked that you wait for her. Can I get you a coffee?" The blonde indicates with a wave of her hand that I'm supposed to sit in one of the large black leather chairs in the waiting area.

"Coffee. Black." I'm irritated by the wait and it's clear in my tone. I have to remind myself it isn't this girl's fault. "Please," I add with an apologetic smile.

Maura making me wait was unusual. She'd only done it once before when she wanted to wear me down. *I really hope for her sake this isn't some sort of game. I am not in the mood.*

The coffee came, as did several other business types, all with appointments, and then they went...and I was still waiting. After an hour, I was in front of the blonde receptionist again.

"Another coffee?" Her eyebrows raised as if there would be no other reason for me to stand in front of her.

"No. I'd like to leave a message for Miss Hearst, please. Can you tell her to call me to arrange another time?"

The ping of the elevator sounded behind me, and with a gush of cold air, Maura swept through reception. "Sapphia, darling. Follow me."

I rolled my eyes and followed her into her office. With one arm out of her coat, Maura hits the button to close the blinds. A whir tells us we'll have complete privacy within ten seconds. The coat gets thrown over the edge of the large brown chesterfield and she turns to face me.

"I've had a fucker of a morning and I desperately need some light relief. Honestly, you take a few weeks' vacation and it all turns to rat shit." Maura smiles. I know it is a smile because it turns the corners of her mouth up and I can see a line of perfectly straight white teeth, but it's as if the message never reached her eyes. "Massage my shoulders for me, will you?" she says, sliding onto one of the wide, low-backed seats.

As if on automatic pilot, I walk round behind her, placing my hands on her shoulders and allowing my fingers to warm her skin through her shirt.

"So how have things been? Tell me about the gym? Are you on target for memberships?"

"Things are going really well. We're beating the six-month projections by a huge margin. I've adjusted the figures for the next two quarters based on what we've done so far and next quarter contains the post-Christmas surge, so I think you'll be impressed."

I was in my wheelhouse and so caught up in telling her about our youth program and the kids' charity Abs had been doing that I hadn't noticed her unbuttoning her shirt. When she pulled my hands down towards her breasts, I jerked them away and stepped back. As she turned to see what had happened, there was a look of utter confusion on her face.

"Sapphy?" Her eyes narrowed as if she was desperately doing her own calculations. "Would you like to tell me what just happened?"

Fuck.

"You can't just disappear for weeks, months on end, and then suddenly come back and expect everything to be the same. I'm not a toy." My words come tumbling out and as I finish, I see what seems to be amusement in her eyes.

"You're right and I'm sorry. Come here." Moving to the edge of the chair, she pats the space she's created. "Sit next to me."

Tugging my hand, she pulls me down next to her. Our bodies are touching, but I place my hands on my lap.

"I've mistreated you. I can see that."

Her aromatic scent fills my senses as she turns her body towards me. It's the same scent she has worn for years. That same familiar intoxicating smell which I have yielded to time and time again. The same scent I'm consumed by now as the warmth of her hand radiates through my top as she rubs my shoulder; as her fingers glide in small circles on the nape of my neck.

"I've met someone," I blurt the words out with more gusto than I intend, but it has the desired effect as it stops her dead.

Her hand is still against my skin. I feel like a possum being eyed by a hawk. If I stay still and hold my breath, she might move on and leave me for dead. In my rational mind I know that's absurd, but the spike in adrenaline coursing through my body isn't supporting rationale thought.

"Who is she?" Maura's tone is neutral.

"Her name is Esha. She works with me at the gym." I squirm as I hear her soft laugh. "This is different, Maura. She's different. I mean, I wouldn't just blow you off unless..."

Unless what? Shit. This was not the time or the place for an epiphany.

Maura's fingers stroked the nape of my neck once more.

"Maura. I can't. I'm sorry."

"But still you don't move," Maura drawled.

I push myself up and walk over to sit on the Chesterfield. Her blouse is still undone. Her firm, tanned breasts pressed against the lace of her bra, her pink nipples clearly visible. I could see them and appreciate their beauty, but the rest of my body did not respond. Not one single twitch. All I could think about is how beautiful Esha's body is, although I'd still to see her naked. I'd held her but never seen her, and there was something even more exhilarating in the anticipation of what might lie ahead.

"Okay." Maura leaned back and buttoned her shirt. "Well, I'm certainly not about to beg. We had an understanding though, and if the nature of our relationship is changing, then so are the terms of the loan."

"You can't—"

"I think you'll find I can and I am. I'm going to give you

exactly six months to repay everything you owe me. If I think our investment is in jeopardy, then I will step in and take over the management."

A pain ripped through my chest. *This is not happening. This can't be happening.*

"Maura, please, you know how much this means to me. It's everything I want. I've put everything I have into making this work. Don't do this," I begged.

Maura closed the space between us and crouched down in front of me.

"Sapphy, you were always my favorite. My champion." Her hand cupped my face and despite myself I felt my eyes grow wet. "You want to play with others in the big bad world then so be it, but that comes at a cost. As my father would say, you can't have your cake and eat it. So what do you want to do? Renege on our deal and keep your little girlfriend or fall back into line like a good girl?"

Rising to her full height in front of me, I felt like a small child who had disappointed a parent.

This is completely fucked up.

"Maura, please. I'm not giving her up. But really what the hell are you going to do with a gym? Please." My voice sounded weak and pathetic. I had gone from almost having everything to now this.

"Please what? Please let me walk over you now that I have everything I want? Please let me take what I want and not hold up our agreement?" The scorn in her voice tore at me. "You've made your choice, Sapphy. When you realize this girl isn't everything you think she is, when she breaks your heart into a million pieces, just like before, you'll be back."

"I'm sorry, Maura." And truly I am, but her words trigger anger inside me. "I'll get your money and you can get someone else to fuck."

Grabbing my jacket, I walk out her office and don't look back.

By the time I make it to my car, I am physically shaking... and lost. I'm still not entirely sure what happened in there. I thought I'd be able to talk to her, to make her understand. I even thought she might be happy for me. How the fuck did I get this so wrong.

For all my bravado, I don't know where the hell I'm going to get such a vast amount of cash from. I'm not even sure I know exactly how much I owe her. The bills kept coming in and like a fool, I never stopped to take stock. I wanted it all, but I never realized the cost. Not the actual cost. And now it was too late. I was losing it all and over what? A school girl infatuation?

FOURTEEN
ESHA

Monday's are always hard. I have three classes, one in the morning, one in the afternoon, and one in the evening followed by a client with rigid TFL that needs soft tissue treatment. But today was especially hard. I know Sapphy was worried about the meeting she had with the investor this morning, and I worry for her. I found her office empty at lunchtime but hadn't been too concerned. Sometimes these things run over. There really was nothing to be concerned about as the business was doing well. Better than well, it was already profitable, and I know from my own experience that isn't easy to achieve for a start-up.

With the towels for the laundry under one arm, I use the other to switch off the light in the treatment room and make my way downstairs to reception. Abs looks up as I pushed through the double doors.

"That, you finished?"

I nod, stuffing towels into the bags ready for the laundry company to pick up in the morning.

"Is Sapphy in? I thought I'd just nip in and see her before I leave for the night."

"She's not been in all day. I'm supposed to be cooking dinner tonight for Hayley and Gracie, but I'm here covering her shift."

"I can cover the last hour for you? I don't mind." I'm shattered, but another hour will not kill me.

"It's sweet of you, but no. I'm in the doghouse now, anyway. I'll pick up some chocolate on the way home. That's guaranteed to win around the women in my life."

"I've never known Sapphy not to be in. Even on a day off, she's in here. Did she call?"

Something was eating away at me. A gnawing feeling in my stomach.

"Not a message, not a call. It isn't like her, but then again she was with Maura today, so shit knows what might have happened." Abs rolls her eyes.

"Maura?" I'd heard that name before, but where? And then it hit me. That awful woman that draped herself around Sapphy at the opening night. Maggie had gone on for what felt like an age about how much she disliked the woman's aura. "Maura is the investor?"

Abs stares at me. "You know Maura? Did Sapphy tell you about her?"

It would have been easy to play dumb and say I knew everything, hoping Abs would tell me more, but I don't play games. Tempting as it might be.

"No, but I was with her till three this morning, helping prepare the figures for her meeting with her investor, but she never mentioned that was Maura," I say feeling a little duped. Maybe she didn't tell me because I didn't ask. "I know how stressed she was about it. I'm worried, Abs. I tried calling earlier and I've left a couple of messages, but she hasn't returned them. I'd really like to check on her. What number is her condo on Long Wharf?"

I knew the building that Sapphy lived in, but I'd never been to her apartment. Abs nodded. I wasn't sure if she was going to give me Sapphy's address or not, and I wouldn't have blamed her if she didn't. It was private information, but given our recent conversations, I could only hope she trusted me and trusted what she saw between me and Sapphy. She lifted a pen and started writing. Ripping off the sticky note, she held it out.

"I'm giving you this because I think you are good for her and if she has had a shit day, then yours is the face she'd want to see. But if she's pissed, you never got it from me. Understand?"

Apartment 505, Mezallow Building, Long Wharf.

"Thanks Abs, I owe you." I walk round the desk and give her a hug. "You're the best."

"Telling you if it goes tits up, I know nothing." She throws her arms in the air and winks.

————

I type in 505 into the entry system and wait. The cold wind whips at me, and the entrance to the building offers no salvation against the elements. I hop from foot to foot to stay warm, leaning in to listen for any activity from the electronic pad. The howl of the wind makes it hard to hear. After what seems like several minutes, I try again. And wait.

Perhaps she's gone out. I stand back and look up at the building. There are rows and rows of windows and balconies that overlook the harbor area. Some have lights on and some don't. There's no way of telling which of the neat little boxes is apartment 505. Perhaps she has company. That wasn't something I'd considered until now.

What if she and Maura are...I should go.

Then suddenly the lights on the silver entry system light up and I dart back into the *relative* shelter of the doorway.

"Hello. Sapphy? Sapphy, it's Esha," I shout loudly, daring to be heard against the howl. I wait for a reply but I don't hear one, instead the door lock clicks open and I'm permitted access.

Beyond the functional, small vestibule, the entrance opens up into a hallway that looks more like something I'd expect from a hotel rather than an apartment building. Although these places are labeled as 'condo's' rather than apartments. I'd always thought the fundamental difference between the two was about $800 rent a month, but maybe I was wrong.

I ride the lift to the fifth floor as shown on the engraved silver sign, and it silently transports me. Stepping out into the long carpeted hallway, I follow the numbers down until I reach 505. Knocking gently on the door, I wait.

When the door opens, I see Sapphy's red-rimmed eyes before she turns, leaving the door ajar. I follow her after closing the door behind me. The place is pristine. Minimalist, spotless and pristine. Nothing is out of place. Even the empty bottle of wine and glass on the coffee table look as if they have been staged for a Harper's Bazaar shoot. It's completely different from my home.

The main living area combines a modern, sleek kitchen where everything is hidden and a large living area offering a floor to ceiling view of the harbor. At night the view is stunning. A huge cream leather L-shaped sofa sits in the center, but it almost seems insignificant in the room's vastness. On the sofa, curled up, lies Sapphy, like the smallest Russian doll. I move to her side and kneel next to where she lies. I've never seen her like this, and from what I know of her character, I'm pretty sure very few others have either.

Stroking her hair I ask, "Sapphy are you okay? What's up?"

I wait, but she doesn't reply. Whatever it is, causes her pain because her eyes squeeze shut and a tear escapes.

"Hey, you can talk to me. Whatever it is, you can talk to

me," I whisper softly. I stroke her hair for a few more minutes, but she says nothing, only tears keep running free. I glance at the bottle and wonder how much she has had.

Was it opened today?

"I'm going to get us a couple of glasses of water, okay?" The lack of handles in the kitchen throws me until I realize everything is 'touch open.' Compared to my house, this place is space aged.

By the time I return with the water and some tissues I'd found in the bathroom, Sapphy is sitting up. She wipes her eyes, then blows her nose with such force I tease her about sounding like a trumpet. She gives a sad light laugh. I don't rush her. Whatever is upsetting her will, if she chooses, come out in time. So I just sit with her. Quietly.

Our breathing aligns. The rise and fall of our chests synchronize. After a short while, I hear a little of the torment leave her body. After several moments, she reaches over and takes my hand. I offer a small squeeze of support. She smiles.

"I've fucked up."

A slight panic rises in me. What has she done? *Has she—? With Maura?* My stomach lurches, but I push it down. *Wait,* I tell myself, *just wait.* Several more minutes pass before she speaks again.

"I going to lose the gym. Everything I've worked for. And Abs and Logan, they left jobs to work there. And you..." Her lips quivers, "I'm so sorry Esha." Tears fill her eyes and then with a blink, they spill forth and she looks away, wracked in what seems like shame.

"I don't understand. We did the projections last night. The business is healthy, you're making money, Sapphy." I shake my head in confusion. None of this makes sense. "And why would you lose me?"

"I made a deal with Maura, for the investment and I can't

anymore, I just can't so she wants it all back. Everything—and I don't have..." her words trail off into silent sobs that convulse through her body. I don't press her, I simply hold her hand. Slowly, she calms again. "I'm sorry. I know I'm not making sense but—"

"Shh, it's okay." My tone is calm and soothing. "Why don't you start at the beginning and take your time. There's no rush." I watch as she nods and inhales deeply, as if steeling herself for what comes next.

Over the next two hours, Sapphy tells me everything. Unfiltered, raw and complete. I hold her hand throughout it all, saying very little but listening intently and nodding in understanding. It's complicated, but I decide my dislike of Maura is the most straightforward element of the night. Sapphy looks tired, drained but most of all, defeated.

"We can deal with this, together. There will be a way out of this. There always is." I drop my head so I'm eye level with her and look directly into her eyes. "Do you trust me?" I ask and she offers me a slow nod.

Tomorrow, we will deal with all of this, especially Maura.

FIFTEEN

I'm up, showered, and making coffee when Sapphy rises. I stayed the night, not wanting to leave Sapphy on her own. I get the impression sleeping in the same bed with someone without the need to have sex is something new to Sapphy. Not that I don't want to have sex with her because I do, and from the way I catch her looking at me, the feeling is mutual. I just want it to be right. It needs to be naturally given at the right time, for the right reasons, and after everything Sapphy confessed last night, it's even more important that we give any physical connection between us the respect it deserves.

My mind has been racing with thoughts of how we can tackle repaying the investment over such a short period. First, we need to tell those that need to know. Second, we need to enlist help. Most of all, we need to figure out how to remove Maura from the picture, while suffering no catastrophic losses. But first I need to see the paperwork.

After nipping out and grabbing some provisions for breakfast, my first call is to Maggie. As a retired lawyer, her expertise might prove useful. I asked her to meet us at the gym at eleven so that gives me enough time to get in, help Sapphy dig out all the paperwork we need and teach my morning class. We can work everything else out from there.

"You didn't need to do all this. Thank you." Sapphy smiles as she sips her coffee. Her hair is still damp from the shower. It looks a little darker, but the slight waves are already taking shape.

"You'd do the same for me." I rest my elbows on the breakfast bar. "I hope you don't mind, but I've asked Maggie to look at the contracts. She's happy to help and I think..." I pause a little, hoping Sapphy will at least consider what I'm about to say next. "If Maggie reckons Maura can really change the terms, then we might talk to Abs and Logan too. We're all in this together and I know they'd want to help if it comes down to that."

"What do I tell them? I pimped my body for the chance of owning a gym and sorry guys, but I've decided not to fuck Maura anymore, so she has fucked me instead. So you'll need to find another job?" She shook her head. "I'm sorry. You don't deserve this. I'm just..." She looks up at the ceiling and I know she's holding back tears. "I'm just so fucking ashamed of myself, Esha. I was so wrapped up in getting *what* I wanted I didn't think about the right or wrongs of *how* I was doing it."

My heart is breaking for her and I want to help, not just because I feel partly responsible for this whole thing. It's because of me that everything has been turned on its head and I can't let her down when she needs me the most.

"You've not let anyone down, Sapphy. You might not have made the best choices," I say with a shrug and a smile, "but this isn't the time for a postmortem. We need to get our shit together and sort this out." I wink at her while playfully thumping the counter, and I'm rewarded with the smallest of laughs. It's not much, but I'll take it.

"Right, finish up and grab your stuff. Today, we take on the world."

———

"I will not lie. It's not good. Maura has the right to change terms or call in the loan at any point, and if you don't have the means to pay it back, she can make moves to take over the business." Maggie shakes her head. "How did your lawyer ever let you sign this," she asks, waving the contract in her hand.

"I didn't have a lawyer," Sapphy mumbles. "She was my friend, and I didn't think I needed one."

Maggie seems to understand and much to my relief, her tone softens.

"For some, like Maura Hearst, there are no friends in business. We might not be able to do anything about what's gone before, but if she wants to change the terms, then that opens the door to revising this garbage and this time I'm going to ask you to let me help you. I'll be your counsel."

Maggie's words seemed to send a wave of relief through Sapphy. I too nod, happy for Maggie's help.

"Do you think we'll need to pay back the full amount within the next six months?" I ask. I know the answer I'm hoping to hear. Within that second, as I wait for an answer, I mentally cross everything, but it isn't the answer I want.

Maggie explains that we have to plan for the worst and consider any additional time she can get as a bonus. Sapphy's head drops. We'd gone through all the papers this morning and including the purchase of the building itself. The total debt is a little over five and a half million. The only silver lining was that Maura's team had done a sterling job on the property negotiations. It was a steal, especially in a rising market, but selling the gym to a developer isn't an option. No, we need to raise cash and fast.

A commercial mortgage could help, but we still required a down payment, not to mention getting Maura her money back. We need to muster the troops if we are to salvage anything from Maura's clutches. We agree to meet again this evening. It'll be a late night, but if we want to bring Abs and Logan in on what is happening, then we have to wait until the gym is closed and everyone has left for the night. This morning has just been one more body blow when Sapphy is already feeling battered.

The knot in my stomach tightens. I would hold all her pain for her, if I could. Right now, she needs people to support her in the same way she has supported all of us.

SIXTEEN

SAPPHY

Esha believes that Abs and Logan will support me, but I don't know if I completely believe her...but I have to remain hopeful.

I don't know what time it is when there's a knock on my office door. I look up to see Esha with a half-smile on her face. "We've closed up. Abs and Logan are waiting with Maggie downstairs. Are you ready to come down?" She extends her hand towards me, an act of support.

I swallow, nodding slowly. "Okay..." I'm not ready, I know that, but I have little choice. If they're waiting for me, I have to show up. So I reach out, take Esha's hand, and we walk down the stairs together.

Esha leads me into the front office, where they are all waiting. Logan is sitting on the corner of the desk; Abs lounges in the chair in front. Concern is clearly etched on both of their faces, and I feel awful for making them worry.

"Are you okay?" Abs asks before I can even sit down.

Esha lets go of my hand and I walk around to the desk chair, taking a seat. She comes to stand behind me, placing her hand on my shoulder and I feel more confident.

"I need to talk to you and I didn't want to be interrupted, so thanks for hanging back. I know you've got better things to do with your time." It's the easiest thing to start off with. It's a hell of a lot easier than coming straight out with what really is wrong.

Abs brow furrows and Logan just looks puzzled.

"What is it?" Abs asks. "Are you ill?"

"No. No, nothing like that."

Abs nods as if that reassurance has taken the edge off her anxiety. I swallow again, a lump forming in my throat. Nervousness builds inside my stomach, making a home there. I don't know how to start it, so I stop thinking about it. I just start talking.

"The investor wants me to pay back the entire investment earlier than planned. They want the entire money returned within the next six months." I can see questions form in their faces. "And I don't have it."

"Why in the hell are they doing that?" Logan blurts out.

Abs catches my eye. She's already figured this out. I look down at my lap, Esha's hand is still comfortingly on my shoulder.

"Maura is pissed you've got together with Esha," Abs says, spitting out the statement. I swear that girl knows me better than I know myself at times. "Fuck, Sapphy don't tell me you were still shagging her when you got her to agree to give you the money for this place?"

Before I can reply, Logan takes over.

"Maura is the investor? You've got it together with Esha? When did—why am I always the last to know shit?"

She now looks both shocked and confused. Guilt floods through me. This is all my doing.

"So let me see if I'm getting this. You are sleeping with Maura and you get this idea to open a gym, so you ask, she

lends and here we are, but at some point you and Esha become
—together, whatever, but you do the dirty on Maura so she
wants her money back. Is that about the size of it?"

"Fuck, Logan, nobody does the dirty on Maura," Abs says,
her voice raised. I can't tell if her frustration and anger are
directed at me or Maura. "Maura uses people, chews them up
and spits them out. She just can't bear to see anyone else happy.
She's like one of those dementors in Harry Potter."

The mention of Harry Potter has us of all staring at Abs.

"What? I've got a bored thirteen-year-old I'm trying to
entertain. Anyway, besides the point. Maura is pissed you
aren't dancing to her tune, and she wants her money. Yeah?"

I don't have to look at Logan and Abs to know that they're
disappointed, that they're ashamed of me, and what I've done.

"What a bitch," Logan says, breaking the silence that settles
over the room. "I knew she was awful, but I didn't imagine she
was that awful."

That's *not* the reaction I was expecting. I slowly raise my
head to look at them and find that the disgust and shame that I
expected to see aren't there.

"She's always been awful. This isn't a new low for her,"
Abs spits.

"You're...not mad?" I ask, looking between the two of them.

"Oh, I definitely think you made a dumbass decision
getting involved with that sort of low life," Logan says before
offering me a gentle smile. "But I can't say I wouldn't have done
the same thing. Like, if I was single and if that were all that
stood between me and my dreams, I might take the risk too."

"We're not mad at you, Sapphy," Abs says.

She gets out of the chair and walks around the desk. Esha
steps aside as Abs wraps her arms around me from behind,
giving me a squeeze.

"You made a mistake that you didn't know would turn out

to be a mistake. I know now isn't the time to say I told you so, but with Maura, *I've told you so*, so many fucking times I've lost count. Maybe this time you'll listen."

I'm so grateful to hear her words. I get choked, and I have to swallow down the emotion, but she isn't finished.

"So how do we sort out this fucker? Sorry." Abs turned to Maggie. "Maggie, I'm assuming that's why you're here?"

When I look up, I see Maggie nod. Logan is on her phone, typing away. "We'll need money, right? I've an idea."

"Already?" Esha asks.

"I recently started seeing this girl, Dani. She's like a PR whizz. Anyway, she has a friend, Beth, who's an investment portfolio expert. I'm checking now to see if we can arrange a meeting. Maybe we're not experts on this stuff, but they are. They can probably help us come up with a better plan. Or at least tell us our options."

"I've been thinking too." Maggie's voice had a certain amount of gravitas to it when she speaks, and without exception, we all stop to listen to what she had to say. "The strength of this place is in its community, how it's bringing people together, giving them a safe place to be. So I was thinking we might look at options to convert it to a cooperative?"

Maggie pauses and seeing the blank looks on our faces, she explains more.

"It's an option where employees and members take over ownership of the business, together, for the good of the community. Your involvement with the youth charities would be safe, which might not be the case if a private investor took over. It might be worth looking into that as an option? I can do that for you if you like?"

"So we might own it together? We could all get involved?" Abs asks, obviously curious. "But where would we get the money?"

Maggie chuckled. "Well, it would take more than just us. Unless one of you is a secret millionaire?"

A beat of silence confirmed the lack of wealth in the room.

"There are some community based financial institutions specifically aimed at offering small loans to help employees and members form cooperatives, so you don't even have to have the money in the bank. You all invest what you can, and your members do the same. Give them an option to invest, and what they invest is reflected in their share of the cooperative. I'm not saying it's certain we can do it, I mean we'd have to get enough buy-in and there's a lot of red tape, but it's worth considering... along with other options, too."

Nods came from everyone around the room. A plan was coming together.

Logan was going to talk to Dani and Beth; Maggie was going to look at exactly what we'd need to get a cooperative off the ground, and Abs was pulling together the full membership information. Although we didn't have a solution yet, sitting here surrounded by friends, I felt supported. Last night I thought I'd lost everything, but tonight these four people in front of me were giving me the most precious thing in the world. Hope.

SEVENTEEN

That night I hadn't returned home to my condo. When the meeting was over, Esha held out her hand yet again and took me to her home. There was something warm and comfortable about her place. It was like getting an enormous hug as you walked through the door. Walking through my front door had a very different feel, one I was glad to avoid for now. My condo was a sharp reminder that my over ambitious lifestyle was crumbling around my ears.

The heating system creaks into life as Esha puts me to work in the kitchen. Standing shoulder to shoulder in front of two chopping boards, we prep the vegetables for dinner. Carving my way through the butternut squash in a methodical fashion, I watched in awe as Esha's quick fingers make light work of the onions. I'm so distracted my knife slips against the smooth outer skin of the squash and searing pain shoots through my finger. I let out a yelp. For the briefest moment I looked at my finger and see nothing, but the pain stops me from looking away and then inevitably comes the vibrant, fluid red that oozes from the almost imperceptible wound.

"You've cut yourself." Esha grabs my hand and leads me to the sink. With the tap running, she gently holds up my hand until the crimson flow slows. "I need to clean it," she tells me, and I silently watch as she dips my finger into the running water. The pain I'd felt earlier is replaced with quiet and a feeling unlike any I've ever felt before. It's replaced with love.

Not the type of love that rises from passion and need, which is so often lust under a cunning guise. No. This is deeper, rounder, as if it has a form within me. *I love you.* I stare at Esha as she peers at my finger.

"It's not deep. You've been lucky. There's too much going on in your head, too many distractions." Esha smiles and lifts her chin up to meet my eyes. Her hand clasps my finger, holding a paper towel in place. She has stopped the bleeding.

Right now though, there is only one thought in my head and that is to kiss her. To place my lips on hers and sink into a long, deep kiss that will let her feel how profoundly she has touched me, touched my heart. Within a single beat, I lean in. My good hand cups the side of her face and when our lips collide with such tenderness, I can hardly breathe. She tastes sweet and warm, and as my eyes flicker closed; I melt into her body.

As our lips part, she guides me through to the long, low chaise longue in the living room. She sits me down and removes the paper towel from my grip.

"Good, the bleeding has stopped," she says, inspecting the cut. "Now remove your clothes."

My mouth falls open. While I have no objection to undressing in front of Esha, her order takes me a little by surprise. Before I can make any enquiry as to why she might want me naked, Esha disappears. So I do as I'm told. Moments later she returns with a large towel and a small bottle of what looks like oil. Suddenly it all makes sense.

"You said remove my clothes, so I did. I removed them all." I shrug, a little unsure if I've done the right thing.

Her mouth forms an 'o' shape and her eyebrows rise along with the corners of her mouth. It's the first time she has seen my body completely, unashamedly naked. Her smile is growing, so I'm assuming she likes what she sees. We've slept together, holding each other, naked, but we've both hidden our modesty in the morning.

"You have a beautiful body." Her hand reaches out and with one finger she traces the outline of my shoulder and down my arms to the inside of my wrist. A ripple of excitement goes through me. "I was just going to give you a massage to release—"

Her breath hitches. Her eyes wandered over my olive skin until they reach my eyes.

She wants me as much as I want her. I close the gap between us and taking her hands in mine; I lift them onto my breasts. They're still cool from the bottle she carried, and my nipples responded immediately. Her thumb flicks over the hard nub, causing me to gasp. All at once she raises her face to mine, sealing our lips together. The weight of her body presses against me, pushing me backwards to the chaise longue. My calves hit the soft velvet padding. I allow myself to fall backwards, widening my legs as Esha almost tumbles on top of me.

As my back hits the soft material, I gaze up. Esha is pulling her tank top and sports bra over her head. Two of the most perfect breasts with dark brown nipples give a small bounce. I'm still appreciating the way they fall, imagining them in my mouth, as she hooks her thumbs into her remaining clothing, pulling them off and discarding them at her feet.

Her body is hot, warm and soft when it hits mine. Our boobs crash together, sending a thrill through every fiber of my being. My mouth is hungry for her, but each time I move forward, she pushes me back. I feel her lips on my chest, my breasts. She sucks my nipple into her mouth and her tongue roughly flicks over the tip. I groan.

Hands – now warm – explore my body, snaking their way down, over my stomach, running over my short hair and my hips twitch. I feel fingers stroke the inside of my thighs in the lightest of touches. They move from my thighs and back up over my mound to my taut stomach. My hips rise to catch her fingers as they graze past the apex of my thighs. Instinctively, my body knows where Esha needs to be, my legs widen so one leg now falls down either side of the wide base. I am giving myself to her fully, begging to be taken.

Sensing my growing need, her eyes glint as they meet mine. She slips down lower, rubbing her skin against my wetness. My body bucks, desperate to push against her. As her hot breath licks against my need, a small cry escapes from my chest.

"Raise your hips for me." Her words are gentle but firm.

Placing one heel back against the velvet, I raise my hips and feel cool air against my wet center. I feel soft fabric rub against my lower back and I lower myself down onto the cushion. She places kisses on the inside of my thigh and then her lips move higher. I feel her warm breath and once again I groan and writhe, desperate for her mouth, her touch. A wet tongue slides down over my clit and my hips rise. I reach down and place my hands on the back of her dark hair. Her tongue is insistent, hungry, and I push hard against her face. My moans are loud. I can't control the need burning inside me.

Fingers delve into my center, in and out, out and in, with each thrust I'm filled more and deeper. Esha's mouth locks over my clit, her tongue relentlessly whipping me. I grip the back of her head harder, pulling her deeper down onto me and my hips slam into her. Her tongue and hand are working in a pounding rhythm. A tingle rises within me and I know I'm about to come.

All I can feel is her inside me, taking me and then in a crash, a shudder, a spasm, I allow myself to fall away.

I pull the cushion from under my hips, throwing it on the floor as Esha crawls up my body in a series of kisses. Her body is hot and I wrap my long limbs around her, clasping her tightly. Her musky scent, her soft skin, the gentle rhythm of her breathing; everything about her consumes me. I never want to let her go.

EIGHTEEN

My office feels far smaller when it's filled with people. The mismatched chairs we've brought from other rooms make the whole thing feel like a bad family Christmas meal without the food, or like some strange AA meeting, given we are all in a circle.

Logan sits astride her chair, which is turned the wrong way round, leaning her arms and chin on the high wooden back. Like the chair, her baseball cap is also back to front and a tuft of short hair sticks out the front. Next to her is Dani, who rests one hand on her girlfriend's leg. Then Beth and Maggie sit next to each other, deep in conversation. From what I gather from Esha, the two of them have been engaging heavily in researching options for the gym. Abs doesn't join in their discussions, instead her head is bowed into her phone and thumbs flick quickly. Something has got her full attention.

Then there is Esha, who sits next to me. A nod of encouragement is sent my way. "You've got this," she whispers just low enough that no one else can hear.

"Everyone," I say, barely loud enough to grab everyone's

attention, but by the time I clear my throat a hush fills the room. "Before we start, I want to say thanks for your time and support. It means a lot."

My voice cracks with emotion and I feel Esha slide her hand into mine and lace her fingers with my own. Intuitively she knows what I need.

"Why don't I bring you all up to speed with my dealings with Maura so far?" Maggie opens the folder which is resting on her lap and slides the glasses from the top of her head down onto her nose.

"Please." I lift my hand, offering her the floor.

Maggie has become my buffer, placing herself between Maura and me, to ensure emotions *don't impede business,* or at least that is how she describes it. I'm grateful for her interventions.

"She is refusing to extend the investment period beyond the initial twelve months, but I have removed the clause where she may send in her own management team to run the business during that period. So while it isn't a brilliant answer, it gives us just over five clear months to raise the capital owed. In that time she cannot touch the business and all communications financial reporting or otherwise will come through me."

Maggie looks round the circle, taking in everyone's serious expressions. For me, just knowing I don't have to sit down and have Maura berate me every month is a tremendous weight lifted off my shoulders.

"Beth and I have had lengthy discussions about the refinancing and potential new structure for the gym which will allow it to operate with a similar mission and premise to its current operations. A cooperative would seem to hold the most promise."

Maggie paused and looked to Beth who, with a nod, picked

up the mantle and ran with it. Between them, they've already formed a tag team.

"As I think Logan has already told you, I have several investment contacts who might snap up the opportunity, but you have to understand exactly what that would look like. For starters, they may decide that the individual assets of the business are worth more than the whole. They might just want the investment because of the potential to develop the site and see the gym as irrelevant to their plans. Even if they want to keep the business as a going concern there is nothing to say they won't want to put in their own management team, or at the very least they could have you jumping through hoops, trying to keep up with their demands for reports and projections. Sapphy, your whole remit would change beyond all recognition. It's just the way these guys operate."

Beth pursed her lips tightly together and let out a long, inaudible sigh before her face seems to brighten.

"But Maggie's suggestion of forming a cooperative is good. I've even got a contact who'd be able to sort out a commercial mortgage if you went down that route, and she's already agreed to waive her fee if you give her free membership." Beth let out a chuckle, and it rippled round the group.

"Are you okay with the membership figures I've given you? Just let me know what you need and I can get it together for you," Abs offers eagerly. "I was talking to Hayley about what was happening and I don't know if you'd go for this, but you know how we've got the extra space that opens out onto K Street?"

She pauses, waiting for me to nod, not that she needs to. It's extra rooms we had developed as part of the renovation, but they're not used. They are fully kitted out, but at the moment all they hold is remnants of packaging and odd bits of excess flooring.

"I thought we might sub-let the space? One of Hayley's colleagues has a daughter who's looking to set up a kid's day care center, and she is struggling to find affordable commercial space and I just thought..."

"That's a great idea, Abs," Dani piped in. "That would sit perfectly with the whole community vibe and might even get us some more members. I can write us a marketing plan, if you, Beth and Maggie could help Sapphy with the business plan?"

Suddenly momentum was gathering.

"So are we doing this then? A community fitness cooperative?" Dani asks excitedly, and we all knew the answer.

"Hell, yes!" is the chorus from the circle.

"Um." Abs raises her finger in the air tentatively. "I just have one question?" She has our full attention. "Am I going to have to teach Zumba?"

Laughter fills the small office. It has never felt so good to be part of a team.

———

There are hugs between us all as we lock up to leave. Abs is heading back, hoping to catch Hayley before she heads out on a night shift; Beth has the promise of a 'sure thing' but when she offers to give Maggie a lift, we all raise our eyebrows undecided about who this sure thing is with.

Dani tries to persuade Esha and I to come out for a late dinner with her and Logan, but I shrug and decline. Esha stays with me while I set the alarm and lock up.

Almost sensing that I don't want to spend the night on my own, she places her head on my shoulder and says, "Come home with me."

There is nothing I'd like more than to spend the night with

Esha curled in my arms, but I need clean clothes, my toothbrush...

"Why don't we nip to your place, grab some stuff and then you can come back with me?"

Esha's question stuns me. *This woman really can read my mind!*

It's exactly what we do, and given we drove in together in my car this morning, it all makes sense. From the moment we sit in the car, we don't stop talking. Esha is even more excited than I am. From being able to offer members the potential of day care to imagining Maggie putting Maura firmly in her place, we discuss everything. It is so easy, as if we've known each other for a lifetime.

I park in my designated space and as we wait for the lift to arrive, I think about everything that I still have to do.

"I need to find somewhere else to rent. The notice to quit here arrived this morning." Esha looks confused. "Maura's company owns this place. She gave me a good deal on it because we—" I couldn't bring myself to say the words. Our arrangements had never seemed seedy or sleazy before, but as I turn the keys in the door to the condo with Esha standing next to me, my past suddenly feels dirty. "I'm sorry. I must be such a disappointment." My chest tightens and I'm frightened to meet Esha's eyes.

Her hand covers mine, and I hold the key still.

"You are not a disappointment to me. You never will be." Esha squeezes her hand tight over mine.

"I'm scared I'm not enough," my admission escapes my lips in a rush and my head drops. "Not enough for you. That you'll realize I've something missing, something wrong with me and leave."

"You're right, Sapphy, you aren't enough for me," a pain crashes through my chest. God, I knew it. As I go to snatch my hand away from hers, she holds it tighter, refusing to let go. "You are more than enough for me. You're more than enough for anyone with a good heart. I will not leave you, I promise."

Reaching up, she places a kiss on the side of my cheek. I believe her.

———

When we swing open the door to the condo, it's cold, dark and empty. I don't want to be here. It hurts. Esha takes my hand and squeezes it.

"Come on, lets grab your things and get out of here."

I grab my holdall from the closet and take it to the bathroom. Esha is sitting on the bed waiting for me. Grabbing my toothbrush and shampoo my mind wanders back to the day we first met, when she walked into the gym and had to climb over half built equipment to reach my office. Would she still have said yes to joining us if she knew then what she knows now?

A chill fills my body, giving me goosebumps as I peel off my leggings to put them in the laundry basket. I brace myself for even more of a chill, pulling my hoodie and top over my head. As I shake my hair free, I give a little jump, suddenly aware of Esha standing in front of me. I hadn't heard her come in.

Her eyes focus on my nipples, which are rock hard with the lack of heat, but the way she is looking at them makes them stiffen a little more. As if shaking herself from her thoughts, her eyes make their way up to mine and for a moment we hold each other's gaze. I'm fairly sure after last night, I know what might come next...but I'm wrong.

"Move in with me." I hear Esha's words, but I'm completely thrown. Interpreting my silence as hesitation she continues. "My house is enormous, way bigger than I need and you can have your own space and I know it's selfish but I like you being there. I know it's fast, but it's not like we've just met and besides, we're lesbians."

A laugh erupts, I can't help myself. This woman is smart, kind, wise, utterly gorgeous, funny and downright adorable, but I can't let her do this.

"Esha I'd love to say yes and I'm pretty certain in a few months or maybe a year it will be a yes. Once I'm back on my feet and I've got something to offer—"

"Then say yes, now. What's the point in being tied into a lease if we know where this is going and you've already given me more than anyone else ever has..." Her eyes lock with mine as if she is looking deep inside me. "You're ready to sacrifice everything for me. Everything you've dreamed of, everything you worked so hard to achieve. I'm not a fool, I know the simple answer would have been for you to have given Maura exactly what she wants, but you didn't and that tells me everything about your heart that I need to know. I know it might seem complicated, with everything that's going on, but what I feel for you isn't. We can be enough together. What do you say?" Her eyebrows rise in expectation.

Wearing only my panties, I shiver and nod. "Okay." I say meekly, "But if you change your mind..."

Her face softens and her eyes smile as she takes me in her arms. "I won't. Now get some clothes on, grab your stuff, and let's go home because it's freezing in here."

"Was it my erect nipples that swung it for you?" I joke, grabbing a clean hoodie from the closet and pulling it over my head.

"Mmm, I'm tempted to cut back on the heating now I've seen the effect."

NINETEEN

ESHA

Over the few weeks I see first Sapphy's genuine fighting spirit come out and my heart sings with pride. She splits her days between managing the gym and meetings to set up the new structure, with the help of Beth and Maggie. I can see her confidence grow every day as we tighten our plans and move towards the cooperative campaign.

The campaign officially launches today and Dani's work in bringing together Sapphy's vision in the context of the broader community to offer *genuine inclusive growth and local economic resilience* has been amazing. I'm using Dani's words because they are so much better than those that Sapphy and I came up with; we described it as empowering women and their health for stronger communities, but Dani's words sounded much more professional and she has found a whole pile of funding and grants which we can apply for, some now and some once we get the cooperative established.

We all gathered around the PC in the front office. Sapphy is sitting in the chair in front of me and I lean forward with my head on her shoulder. Abs and Logan press against my shoulders as we all watch the screen.

"Are we ready?" Sapphy asks, her finger poised on the return key.

"Go for it," I whisper in her ear.

"Will you just push the damned button," Abs says through a mix of excitement and frustration.

Sapphy giggled and hit the return key, and in that moment through the wonders of technology (set up by Dani) we send a personalized email out to every one of our members, inviting them to join our cooperative. Step one is complete and we all look at each another.

"Well, we've done it now." Logan ran her fingers through her short hair. "We better start putting our mouths where our money is and convince them to invest."

The fizz of excitement in the room is palpable and a huge grin erupts on all our faces. Sapphy had a vision to empower women, and it has started with us. We were taking control and giving everyone the opportunity to be part of what we're building. A shared vision, a united purpose. It feels so good.

In the months I've known Sapphy, I've always regarded her as remarkable, but never more so than right now. Her dream is now our dream, and she is sharing it with us all.

The audible ping tells us we've got mail.

"It'll be of those undelivered notification things you get. I bet half our members have changed their email addresses already," Logan mutters as she checks her watch. "I've got to set up for a class. If anything earth shattering happens, let me know."

"Logan, you can be such a cynic." Abs bumps Sapphy's shoulder. "Well, check it then."

Sapphy hovers over the unread email. I can tell she's nervous. We talked about this before coming in this morning.

What if no one wants to be part of it? What do we do then? It is the first time since that night I visited her condo and found her in tears that I'd seen doubt creep in. I place my hand on her shoulder and squeeze. It's okay to have pre-match nerves.

With one click of her right index finger, the email opens. I lean forward eagerly reading the response, as did Abs, and we all let out a cry of delight when we realized we had our first official cooperative member, well except for our little core team.

The next hour more and more emails came in and the phone started ringing. I left Sapphy and Abs to hold the fort to teach my morning yoga class, almost unable to contain my excitement. We'd all agreed to start the classes of this week with a bit of a sales pitch about the benefits of being part of the cooperative, and this was going to be my first shot at converting a few hearts and minds.

Beth had calculated that based on the minimum buy-in figures, if we converted 65% of those that attended the gym into cooperative members, then we'd have enough money to pay back Maura.

Every single woman counts.

I give my pitch, which lasted only a few minutes, and try to start my class, but everyone is more interested in asking questions about how they can get involved. I end up marching them all to the front office so they can sign up. The look on Sapphy and Abs faces as twenty women descend upon them is priceless. And my experience isn't isolated. We've inadvertently stumbled across something that is capturing people's imaginations.

It's all hands to the pump the first few days, and between us we are either teaching or signing up new cooperative members. Logan is sitting at the front desk when I finish my second class of the day, and she offers a smile when she sees me.

"Can you believe this? I've spent most of the morning out

here talking to people about the co-op option and apart from one really grumpy woman who evidently got out of bed on the wrong side this morning, everyone is signing up or promising to sign up. We've run Sapphy off her feet the whole day."

"I'll call Maggie and see if she can come in and help us," I suggest.

"Dani and Beth have offered to come in for the next few evenings, so if Maggie could help during the day, she'd be a lifesaver." Poor Logan really did look stressed, but it was for the best reasons we could have ever hoped for.

Maggie agreed to come in the next day, and every day for as long as we needed her. I will have to take her for lunch to say thank you as soon as we have time. She might be sixty-eight, but she is a force of nature and it would appear I'm not the only one who thinks so because when we go to leave at the end of the night, Beth is once again giving Maggie a ride home. Nobody says a word, but we all exchange small smiles.

TWENTY

The next day, as soon as we walk through the doors of the gym, Abs is waiting with a huge grin.

"You okay?" Sapphy eyes her suspiciously.

"Yeah, I'm good." She lets Sapphy head on up to her office and then nods me into the front office behind reception. She has a smile on her face, a knowing one, and turning to the door she makes sure no one is about to walk in before she speaks.

"You can't tell Sapphy," she starts. "Promise?"

This feels like a double-edged sword. I shouldn't be keeping things from Sapphy this early in our relationship...but this doesn't seem like something *bad*. Abs seems excited.

Tentatively, I nod. "Okay...what am I not telling Sapphy?"

She looks around us again, just to make sure that we're alone. "Logan just told me that Dani has the interview on the radio. It's with 99.7 FM at that!"

My eyes widen. 99.7 is the most popular radio station in the city. They have billboards all over; they do constant fundraisers and local events to get people involved. If they were to stop broadcasting, I think our community would riot.

"Seriously?" I feel excitement building within me. This is a wonderful thing. There's just one thing I cannot figure out. "Why are we not telling Sapphy that?"

"We're going to surprise her! We're going to play the broadcast over the intercom system. She needs something good to happen."

I agree. Sapphy has had a rough time and although yesterday was an impressive start, we've still got a small mountain to climb. She was on a high last night, but utterly exhausted from the emotional overload she's been going through.

"Okay," I say, nodding. "I will keep it a secret, but when is the interview?"

"In just a few minutes. Dani evidently got on during the radio station's peak morning time!" The excitement is radiating off of Abs and I feel it too. This is just huge for our community and I love it.

The wave of hopefulness that I've been feeling these last few days continues to grow.

"Okay!" I say with excitement. "I'm going to go find Sapphy and make sure she's going to pay attention."

"Bring her down here! That way we can all listen together!" Abs calls to me before I head towards Sapphy's office.

Just as I thought, Sapphy is sitting at the desk, staring at the computer in front of her. She runs a hand through her dark hair, sighing. She doesn't notice me as I enter the room, only noticing when I close the door behind me. She jumps slightly before a smile creeps over her features when she sees me.

"You just can't keep away, can you?" she teases.

"There might be a little truth in that." I walk over and sit on the edge of the desk, watching as she types away at the keyboard again.

"Feeling like we need a secretary. Every time I finish one email reply, my unread emails have jumped by five. It's great, but I'm still not sure it's enough to pay Maura back—"

I cut her off by reaching down and taking her hand in mine. "Breathe," I tell her. "Everything will work out, I swear. You can't expect it to all fix itself in just one day."

"I can hope, though." She offers a smile on her face, which leaves me laughing.

"Yes, yes. Anyway." I turn to glance at the clock in the corner of her computer screen. "Come with me for a minute."

"Esha," she says, looking at our hands. "I'm a little busy right now. I'm sorry but—"

"Sapphy, trust me. You are going to want to come with me." I hold out my hand to her.

I watch as she seems to think over it for a minute before finally deciding to take it. I lead her down the stairs and into the front office, where every staff member, who isn't currently teaching, has gathered.

Sapphy arches an eyebrow. "What's this? Is this an intervention because I've been stressing out so much? I promise you guys that I'm okay."

Abs laughs. "It's nothing like that, Sapphy. Just take a seat, okay?"

Her eyebrow stays raised as she walks over to one of the office chairs and slumps down. I sit on the edge of the desk alongside Logan, and Abs sits behind it.

Abs turns to look at Logan. "Tell me when?"

"Texting her now."

Sapphy looks over at me. "Esha, do you want to tell me what's going on? Because it's really feeling like a type of intervention."

"Sapphy." I laugh. "Be patient and trust us."

"Patience is not a virtue that I currently have, Esha."

I lean forward so I can whisper in her ear. "Then it is one I will teach you later."

Then I watch with amusement as Sapphy's cheeks turn red.

Abs is fiddling with something at the desk, trying to connect our check-in tablet to the small intercom system installed in the gym. When she finally gets it, she gasps in excitement before pressing another button.

Before Sapphy can ask what's going on for the hundredth time (not that I blame her), the familiar sounds of 99.7 FM's intro music blare over the speaker.

"Sorry, sorry. I'm turning it down," Abs says, turning it down from blaring.

"Why are we listening to the radio?" Sapphy asks.

"Good things come to those who wait." Logan grins at her, resulting in Sapphy looking even more frustrated with the answers she's receiving.

"*Good morning!*" declares the host, a man in his late forties called Arnie. "*You're listening to 99.7 FM, your number one station for music and fun! As you all know, we here at 99.7 love to give back to our community, and today, we have a special guest here to help us. So, please give Dani Rooney a welcome!*"

"*Thank you, Arnie.*" Dani's voice comes over the radio. I watch as a smile pulls over Logan's face as she hears Dani's voice. Sapphy, on the other hand, is still exchanging confused looks.

"*So, Dani, what is it you're here to tell us about today?*"

"*Well, Arnie, I'm here to talk about the new gym that opened downtown at the corner of East 1st and K Street. If you've been in that area, I'm sure you've all seen it, right?*"

As Dani speaks, I see realization dawn over Sapphy's face. Her eyes light up in shock.

"*The gym's been a colossal hit,*" Dani continues, "*and that is mainly down to the ethos of the woman whose brain child the whole thing was. Sapphia Adamos. Now if you've ever heard of mixed martial arts, Taekwondo, boxing, Jiu-Jitsu, then you'll have heard her name. It's by women, for women. A safe space where you can improve your fitness, your confidence, and be supported. And it isn't just for women who are already fit, it is for every woman in the community, regardless of age, size, or experience. It's for all women. I joined after being attacked in the street for my wallet. I wanted to defend myself, to be less frightened, so I joined their Krav Maga self-defense classes and the difference it has made to my life has been immeasurable and I'm also the fittest I've ever been.*" Dani gave a chuckle. "*But that's just a side benefit. We've women who suffer from anxiety who benefit from our yoga and meditation programs, domestic abuse survivors who, through fitness, are rebuilding their lives. And lots of women who just want to feel better about themselves.*"

"*I get the gym is a great place, Dani, but tell me, why you are here today? Is this just advertising to sell gym memberships?*"

"*No, it's not Arnie, and thanks for asking. Since the gym has opened it has become part of the community and we want it to become even more embedded in the community, so we are turning it into the first women's fitness cooperative in the city. We're inviting all the women in the city to come together and support each other, improve their own lives and those of other women by buying into the cooperative. Help us build a better future for all women by investing and owning together. And it isn't just your own future you are investing in. We have charitable youth programs for teenage girls, offering them chances for the future they'd never have had before. Installing confidence and greater self-esteem. New day creche facilities are coming along too, Arnie. I could spend your entire show telling*"

*everyone why they should become part of this new fitness coop-
erative."*

*"Wow. You're telling me people can own a part of the gym?
Their opinions will actually matter?"*

*"Absolutely. This may have started as Sapphia Adamos's
vision, but she has been generous enough to share that with all of
us. Her vision was to empower women and what better way is
there to empower than by giving them ownership."*

*"So if we have women out there who are listening to this and
want to get involved, how do they do that?"*

*"We have several ways you can get involved. You can come
down and see the gym and meet Sapphia herself or you can go to
our website, where we have a number of options, you can sign up
to join the gym, opt to join the cooperative or if you don't feel
that is for you but you believe in what we are doing, then we are
also taking donations through our crowdfunding page. Together,
we can make a real difference Arnie and who knows, maybe in
time there will be fitness cooperatives in every city and we can
spread Sapphia's dream."*

I turn my attention away from the broadcast, looking over
at Sapphy who seems like she's on the verge of tears. She
looks unbelievably happy and I feel my own emotions
overflow.

"Thank you very much, Dani," Arnie says. *"So, you all
heard it here. The website you need to visit will be our featured
site of the day here at 99.7 FM, so make sure you check it out.
Now, let's head across to Mike for the latest city traffic and travel
updates."*

Abs clicks off the radio, and all eyes are on Sapphy. Tears
are running down her cheeks, a smile clear on her face. She
looks amazed and in awe of what just happened, and if we're
being honest, I am as well. Dani was so natural, nobody could
have done a better job.

"I don't know what to say," Sapphy finally says, looking around at us.

"You don't have to say anything," Abs says. "This is for all of us. This may have started out as your dream, Sapphy, but it's becoming a collective dream for all of us. We want to see this thrive just like you do. We're in this together."

She uses the heel of her hand to wipe at the tears. "I swear, I don't usually cry this much. This has just been one hell of a week."

I laugh, leaning over to kiss the side of her head. "It is okay to cry, Sapphy. All of our emotions are running high. Right?" I look around the room and everyone nods in agreement. "It's good to let it out."

"We wanted to surprise you with this. Now we're really going to have people's attention," Logan pipes in, looking down at her phone, likely responding to Dani.

"I don't know how I'm going to stay on top of all this."

"You're not," Logan says after a moment. "Dani's got some of her team to help, and Maggie and a few of her friends are all coming in to help too. We're a team." Logan gave Sapphy a hug. "Right, well, I'd better go and get beaten up by my Sixty Plus Krav Maga class." Hearing us all laugh, she too joins in. "You have no idea. They just don't hold back!"

One by one everyone heads back to work, leaving just me and Sapphy.

"I've no idea what to say to everyone. And to you." She takes my hands and pulls me down onto her lap. "I'm not sure I deserve all this."

"We're all here for you, and each other. Did you ever really doubt how much people loved you?"

It still dumbfounds me she can't see in herself what we see.

"I think I needed all the false stuff to be stripped away so I could see what really matters." She blushes. "I'm sorry I'm not very good with trying to explain. I just know you've helped me see things, feel things. You've changed everything Esha, and I love you for it."

I lean in and kiss her with more passion than what a thousand words could ever say.

TWENTY-ONE

SAPPHY

I'm overwhelmed by how much everyone is coming together to help. I know they said that they would, and it's not like I don't have faith in my friends, but I didn't imagine them creating this whirlwind around us.

After the radio interview with Dani, the website crashed, unable to cope with the volume of visitors. Emails continue to come, and calls, and I'm so grateful for Dani, Maggie and all the people who are pitching in to help. Each time I try to sit down for five minutes, I get a call from reception to tell me there's somebody else who wants to talk to me. The last few months have just been madness.

Dani had what she's christened as the 'cooperative accumulator' placed in reception. It's basically a large LED screen that she had kicking around her PR office, which is now attached to our foyer wall. Everyday we update the accumulator figure to reflect what we've raised, and it gives us all that extra boost to keep going. The biggest jump in the total came in the weeks after Dani's initial radio appearance, and then again when the local TV station came to interview us as part of their evening news bulletin. Dani held my hand through the whole thing, assuring me I was doing great, but I felt like a bunny in headlights for most of the entire four minutes it lasted.

There's only a matter of days left before we have to meet Maura's deadline, and we still have a way to go to reach the total amount she wants repaid. We raised enough for the down payment on the commercial mortgage. I hadn't appreciated how hard it was to get a mortgage as a cooperative, but Beth's contacts and savvy have got everything in place for us, as soon as all our funds are there. We've even raised all the funds to pay back all the renovation money. It's just the interest Maura is applying, which we're still battling to raise.

To have come so far I can't believe we might not make that last hurdle, but I will not stop trying.

I don't know what time it is when Esha opens the door to the office and steps aside, coming up to the desk and leaning against it.

I look up at her. "Am I late for something?" I turn to glance at the time on my monitor, suddenly realizing it's now 8:00. It's time to stop for the day. I look back at my inbox, seeing there are still more emails to respond to. My mouth forms an 'o', as I look up at her.

"Oh" is all I say.

Esha smiles and extends a hand. "I understand you're busy, but it's time for you to take a break. Hovering over a computer all day is not good for you."

"I just need to answer back a few more emails."

"If they are as interested as they seem, they will still reply in the morning."

She's trying to pry me away from the computer, and I know I should follow. But I can't walk away. I want this so badly. "Esha," I try to argue, but she drops her hand and comes around the desk.

Reaching out, Esha grabs the arms of the desk chair and spins me around so I'm looking at her. I try to turn and look back at the computer screen, but Esha snaps her fingers, causing me to jump.

"Please, Sapphy," she says softly. "I need you to take a break. It will be good for you. I promise that in the morning, everything will still be there for you to work on. We will get back to everyone tomorrow and see where we're at with members. Okay?"

Esha speaks more firmly than I have ever heard her before. It's a gentle demand, one that I can't help but follow. I sigh. "Alright. Just let me log off for the night."

"I am going to stand here and watch you."

It's hard not to find it endearing as Esha stands behind me, arms crossed over her chest, making sure I close everything down. It feels wrong. I feel like I should respond to all the emails. The quicker I do so, the quicker I get Maura off all our backs.

I haven't spoken or heard from her directly in months. Maggie has handled all communications and I hope she realizes how grateful I am for that intervention. Initially Maura had sent me a few messages demanding we negotiate in person, but she backed off when she realized Maggie was going nowhere fast.

Once I log off, I turn back to Esha who's offering me a smile. "Thank you," she says, extending her hand again.

"Thank you," I say, taking her hand to stand out of the chair. "For everything."

"Enough. Let's just go home."

There is a warm, excited feeling when she says those words. Even though we've been living together for almost five months now, it still makes me feel excited. Happy.

Anyone else would have walked away from this whole situation; from me and the chaos I created, but not Esha. She saw something in me I didn't even know was there. A capacity to love fully.

———

I'm still getting used to saying 'our' home and I when I make a mistake and say Esha's place, she is always the first to correct me. It is *our* home, she reminds me. *Our home.*

Each night we cook together, although I chop and Esha cooks. It's with the same grace she practices yoga, that she moves around the kitchen. I'd never have thought it possible to make something as simple as grabbing ingredients look elegant, but she does.

We fall into silence as we eat, enjoying each other's company and the food. When I finish my dinner, I break that silence.

"Esha, I'm not sure what we'll do if we can't raise the full amount we need."

It's something that has been praying on my mind for the last couple of weeks, which I suppose isn't surprising given the looming deadline, but this is the first time I let those fears have a voice.

It feels strange for me to even acknowledge the self doubt. For years as a fighter, a champion, they taught me to rise about the self doubt, ignore it and overcome it. That's a grand theory if you keep winning, but it will crucify you when you lose. With Esha's help, I'm trying hard to talk more about how I feel. The good and the bad, and as my eyes meet hers, I know she understands how hard it is for me to make that admission.

Reaching across the table, she takes my hand. "We might not win every battle Sapphy, and we might not win this one, but that has always been true." She considers her words. "I have one question for you. If we don't win this battle, will we have lost everything? Are there other things you have gained on this journey which might be a bigger prize?"

There, in that moment, I know she is right. It is what I love about her. With Esha, life is about the journey and not the goal. With a simple question, she allows me to see the world in another way; a bigger, fuller and more positive way; a way in which *I* am of less significance.

"I have so many things I'm grateful for and before all this I'd have taken it all for granted, not giving them a second thought. But most of all, I am grateful for you and what you've taught me."

"What have I taught you?" Esha's voice is curious, she isn't looking to gain a compliment. Instead, the question arises from the fact she is so beautifully unassuming.

"That I don't have to fight for everything in life. That sometimes just quietly asking the world to work with me is all I need to do." My words bring a blush to her cheeks. "But my next question isn't for the world. It's just for you." I pause as I see the curiosity in her face. "Will you let me take you to bed?"

I lead the woman I love up to *our* bed. The soft moonlight falls gently across Esha's body as I undress her. I am learning to take my time over things that really matter, to savor the power of connection, and that is exactly what I am doing now.

I sweep her hair away for the dark skin on her shoulders and plant small light kisses in its wake. Although the room is warm, her body shivers underneath my lips. I grab the hem of her tank top and lift it up and over her head, lifting it high to allow her dark hair to spill freely. Discarding the top, I turn my attention to her slender arms and pull her close; she is both fragile and powerful all at once. The heady scent of amber and jasmine fills me as I close my eyes and inhale deeply.

My flattened hands stroke the perfect curves, from the

small of her back up soft skin until I reach the smooth fabric of her sports bra. I pull that too, over her head. Her breasts fall gently, and as I take a step back to take them in my hands, her dark nipples stand to attention, rough and firm against the flick of my thumb. My lips kiss her neck as I continue to caress her breasts. Everything about her is exquisite.

I feel Esha's hands roam slowly over my sides in featherlight glances and my breath hitches with excitement. This woman is barely touching me, yet the effect she has on me is remarkable. It's almost as if she can reach inside me and touch my soul. Every sinew of my being comes alive in her presence and alights to her touch.

She tugs my tank top over my head, revealing my naked torso. A smile dances on her lips as my own nipples yield to her presence, making no attempt to hide their need. Her dark eyes meet mine and an arousal beyond anything I have ever experienced explodes through my body. I release a low audible moan as she takes my nipple into her mouth, sucking gently. My head falls back, mouth opens, and my eyes flutter closed.

The rising hunger in my body is primal. I need her, all of her. Reaching down, I cup her chin in my hand and tilt it up so I can place my lips against hers and then in one swift movement, I lift and place her gently on the bed. Kissing my way down her stomach, I linger over her belly button, allowing my tongue to make small circles around the indent. Her giggles please me. My thumbs hook into the waistband of her leggings and slide them from her body, along with her underwear. Naked, vulnerable and with such honesty she lies in front of me and I bow to her beauty.

I hastily remove the rest of my own clothes and glide my body over hers. I swear there are sparks as the heat of our skin melds together. My thigh slips between her legs and with a slow rhythm, I grind my body against her heat. We move together, finding a matching tempo until we are no longer two but one connected in mind, body and soul.

"Can I—," I hesitate. I'm torn between asking for what I want and fear of losing this moment, this connection. Is it possible I can have both?

"What is it?" Her dark eyes scour my face, searching for an answer.

"I'd like to...would you like it if I—" I close my eyes and kiss her collarbone. Try as I might, I can't seem to find the words. What we have is so pure it's almost as if I am frightened to sully it by my question.

"Sapphy, whatever it is, just say it." Esha hooks her leg around my middle and pulls me in tight so she can kiss me. "There is nothing you can say just now that will make me love you any less."

Being tight against her warm body, skin on skin, desire on desire, gives me the courage I need. "I bought a toy but I don't know if you would—"

Esha's soft giggle halts my fumbling words. "I'm intrigued. What did you buy?" Her hand is again sliding against my back in long light strokes and I blush like a teenager. "Will I like it?" she asks.

"I hope so." I'm surprised at how bashful I am. "I wasn't sure if I should wait and we could've picked one together, but—"

"Show me." Even in the dim light of the moon, her smile is radiant.

I climb off the bed and pull open the closet, pulling out the dildo and harness. I hold it up and shrug with a slight awkwardness. Pulling herself up and resting against the pillows, she beckons me to sit next to her.

"You are very cute when you're embarrassed," she murmurs, placing a kiss on my cheek.

My fingers fiddle with the black silicon in my hand and it springs into life with a long continuous buzz, causing us both to laugh. "I wasn't expecting that," she said, stroking my cheek.

I'm trying to find the button to switch it off as Esha moves. Straddling my lap, she puts her fingers under my chin, tilting it up to meet her eyes.

"Don't turn it off," she murmurs with the slightest shake of her head.

Reaching over to the top drawer of her nightstand, she pulls it open and selects a small bottle. Clicking the lid open, she settles her weight onto my lap once more and takes my hand, squeezing a small clear blob onto the tips of my fingers.

"I want to play." Her smoldering dark gaze is fixed on me and I can't look away as I rub the lube over the shaft of silicon.

My hand reaches between her legs, fingers sliding between her folds, and her body lifts and falls. Reaching behind me, she holds onto the bedstead and her nipple grazes my cheek. I turn my face, allowing it to slide between my lips. My fingers slide down either side of her engorged clit, and as my thumb grazes the hard tip of her swelling, I ease inside her, deep into the depths of her core. Together, our moan fills the room.

"Rub it against me."

I place the tip against her clit and watch as her head falls back. Watching her submit her body to the pleasure I can bring is beyond intoxicating. My fingers slide out and allow the vibrations to follow their path. I make a pattern of small circles with the end of our new toy before sliding it in and out. I widen my legs a little, spreading Esha's core and adjust my own position so the base of the dildo rests against me, building my excitement too.

Her hips move slowly, as if teasing and then pushing her stomach down and towards me she lowers herself fully, pressing the intense vibrations against me. A jolt of excitement rips through my body, my head spins, my heart is bursting. My mouth latches onto a nipple, my free hand on the small of her back, and I pull us close together as she rises up and down, down and up on the full length inside her.

I have never been so consumed with desire, hunger, love. Small beads of sweat run down her chest and I release her nipple to lick them, burying my face between her breasts. Her movements grow faster, wilder, and she slams herself down into my lap. I pull away a little, so I can see her. Her head is back, long dark hair bouncing in time with her breasts.

"Esha, look at me. Look at me," I repeat my words with a firmness of tone that surprises even me, but she does as I ask.

Deep, dark brown eyes look straight into my own and she gathers pace further and I know she is on the very edge. Her tight grip moves to my shoulders, short nails digging deep into my skin as she pounds down against me, and then in one beautiful moment she gives herself completely to the orgasm. We lock our eyes wide open. Breath strangles inside her body. A thousand fireworks release within me, filling my chest, deafening my ears and suspends me in brilliant light. Together, we find our breath, and as we return to the moment, our hot, sweaty flesh rests heavy against each other.

"I love you," she whispers in my ear, "completely."

I love you too.

TWENTY-TWO

Launch Day minus two. That's what I've called today. It's two days before Maura's imposed deadline. Our team has gathered. Esha and I sit across from Beth and Dani, with Maggie to my left. We're just waiting for Logan and Abs to join us so we can start.

A strange calm nestles inside me and the smile I give Esha is filled with certainty. Certainty that no matter what comes next, we will all be okay. Gone is the shame and self loathing that filled me when we all sat together for the first time, and that feels good.

In a rush of air and apologies, Logan and Abs burst through the door and join us. Beth flicks her hair away from her face and opens a manila folder. "Alright, I guess we should go straight to business. We have a lot to discuss."

I look at everyone else's faces. They look nervous and a palpable tension fills the air. I need to say something. "Before you start Beth, can I just say a few words?" I pause for a breath, just long enough for Beth to nod. "I just want to say no matter what Beth is about to tell us or what happens in the next few days, I need you all to know how much I appreciate you all. I couldn't have asked for a better group of people, friends, to share this—adventure with. Anyway, I just wanted to say that. Sorry, Beth."

They receive my words with nods and small, tight smiles. Everyone is eager to hear what Beth has to say, and only I already knew what she is about to say.

Beth looks around to see if we're paying attention. When she's assured that we are, she starts. "So, I've pulled all the figures together, from the crowd funding page, the donations, cooperative buy-ins, and here is where we are as of 10:00 this morning."

A hush fills the room, and no one dares breathe. Beth's dramatic pause is so long that Dani reaches over towards the papers, only to have her hand be smacked away by Beth.

"Stop with the stalling. Just tell us what we're at," Dani squeals in exasperation.

"I was getting to it! I was building suspense!" Beth laughs, picking up the stack of papers and holding them tightly to her chest. She looks at the first paper. "So, I sorted the data into funding areas and what we will allocate to each to allow us to complete the conversion to a cooperative. As you all know, the down payment on the mortgage for the building is secure and Capital One, have all the paperwork in place to move as soon as we are ready. Between the crowdfunding and the cooperative buy-in from all of us, the other employees, members and the community, we can pay back all the money which we owe for the renovations."

Beth's words receive excited shrieks around the room. She exchanges a quick glance with me. We'd had a call first thing this morning where she gave me a heads up on what she had to say. I nod for her to carry on.

"Regarding the interest payment on the payback of the

investment the monies we have gathered via a small community fund loan and some additional donations have covered approximately 50% of what Hearst Investment have stipulated we need to pay to enable the conversion into a cooperative to take place." Beth swallows and looked down at her papers.

"So what does that mean?" Abs asks.

If she hadn't already guessed the look on Dani and Maggie's faces says it all.

"It means we are about $138,000 short." It's all I've been thinking about since Beth told me, but saying the words out loud in front of everyone made that figure seem even bigger. We are so close but...

"We've still got two days to go, right?" Logan reminds me so much of me. I could almost hear her inner voice shouting, *keep fighting!*

Beth nods, but there is an air of disappointment in the room. We've all put in every cent we have, every ounce of energy, but we've come up short.

"Logan, you're right we have two days left and Lord knows I think we'll all be hoping for some secret investor to drop in a bundle of cash right at the last minute, but I think we may have to accept that it's unlikely to happen now." My heart feels heavy as I see the crestfallen faces of my friends. "There is one last thing I'm going to try. I'm going to speak to Maura."

Esha can't hide her distress.

"I'm coming with you." Maggie thumps down heavy on the arm of her chair with her fist, to an almost comical effect, but nobody laughs.

"No Maggie, I appreciate the offer, but this is something I need to do on my own. This is between Maura and I." I know what I'm saying is right. "I might win her round. Appeal to her *better* nature."

The snort that fills the room comes from Maggie, the one

person who knows how demanding and manipulative Maura can be when the mood takes her. "That woman doesn't have a better nature."

"Look, it has to be worth a try. In the meantime, who knows, maybe a rich benefactor with a spare $138,000 will suddenly appear and if they do someone, please call me." I laugh not because I think the idea is ridiculous, but to shield me from the fact that my joke feels like the last hope.

"I'm going to call her now and see if she'll see me." I leaving them all sitting, and I head to my office to get a little privacy.

"Sapphy."

I'm at the bottom of the stairs when I hear Esha's voice.

"Sapphy, you don't need to do this." Her eyes are pleading with me.

"Esha, I do. After everything that everyone has done, everything they have given, I owe them this. I can't let us come this close and then fail because I didn't have the courage to finish what I started. If anyone can win Maura round, it's me." I shrug.

Esha knows I'm right. If there is anything that can get Maura to cut us some slack, it can only come from me.

"Esha, do you trust me?" My question is simple enough and so too should be her reply, but there is a split second hesitation that leaves me shaking my head.

"I do trust you. I trust *you* completely. It's her I don't trust." She reaches out and places her hand on my arm. "Sapphy, please don't let her make you believe you've done anything wrong or that you're responsible for everyone else. You're not. We made a choice to be part of this."

I know she's right, but my head is already running through what I need to say to Maura. I nod and turn, making my way up to my office.

TWENTY-THREE

ESHA

I watch as Sapphy leaves the office, throwing her jacket on as she walks out. My heart is pounding in my chest, nervousness building. Sapphy has come such a long way in the time I've known her, and there is no one I trust more in the world.

But I also know the type of person Maura is, partly through what Sapphy and Maggie have told me of her and partly from what I witnessed in the brief time I met her months ago. In this world, I have to believe that everyone is good. I need to trust we are all trying our best, even when it's difficult to understand, but I am not a fool. Occasionally in life we are challenged by people who would rather knock us down so we can share their pain. They feel nothing but jealousy for our happiness. Maura is one of these people and my instinct is to protect Sapphy, but that is not for me to do. I must allow this to run its course and just hope that Sapphy's strength will keep her safe.

I make my way up to Sapphy's office. I suppose it is my way of being near her. I almost laugh at myself. What do I think I can do? Channel my positive energy through her keyboard so she can feel me in the room with her?

Leaning back in her big leather chair, I cross my legs beneath me and close my eyes. I need to stop my mind from thinking. Overthinking. I focus on my breath, inhaling deeply in through my nose and then slowly out through my mouth. I let my shoulders fall and relax.

Just as I feel my heart rate slowing, there's a knock at the office door.

It feels like it would be too weird to say 'come in', as it's not my office. But through the glass I see Abs. She reads my smile and comes into the room, bursting with excitement. She's bouncing on the balls of her feet, either anxious or full of energy. Knowing Abs, I'm going to assume the latter.

"Hey! Where did Sapphy go? Beth has just got some news and says Sapphy is going to want to hear this."

"She's gone to see Maura."

Abs's face falls. The energy that was just radiating from her vanishes. Her nose wrinkles and for a moment, all she says is "Oh."

I feel like I have to defend Sapphy's decision. Not that I think Abs is judging her, but because I don't want anybody to get the wrong idea. "She believes she can convince Maura to take the money that we have raised so far and let it all go."

"Do you think that Maura's going to listen?"

I sigh, raking a hand through my hair. I don't know what to say. "I don't know, Abs," I finally answer. "I can only hope that what Sapphy believes is right."

Abs seems to sense my nervousness. She reaches out and places a hand on my shoulder. "Sapphy will be okay, honestly. She's maybe made questionable decisions in the past, but in the last year she's really changed and she loves you Esha. More than you know."

I appreciate Abs, and it's obvious why she has always been Sapphy's right hand. "Thanks, Abs."

She gestures with her head downstairs. "Should we go see if Beth will spill the beans without Sapphy being around? She seemed super excited."

We go and find Beth dragging Logan with us. She is sitting in the front office with Maggie and the two of them are laughing hard. They seem jubilant.

"Bad news," Abs says, interrupting their conversation without a second thought. She doesn't do it crudely. She just does it...very Abs-like. Like she's one of those friends who cannot keep silent. She has to say what is on her mind. When she says 'bad news' though, they stop their conversation and turn to look at her. "Sapphy's already left to speak to Maura."

"Shit. She doesn't need to." Beth sighs and looks towards Maggie, who is just shaking her head. "I wanted to say it with Sapphy here, but...we have the rest of the funding, or at least the promise of it. It's enough to secure a short-term loan for the difference."

"What are you talking about? How? I thought we were still $138,000 short?" Logan says, pushing off from where she was leaning against a desk. She stands up straight, with her arms crossed over her chest. "Did we get a miracle donor?"

"Not quite. I applied for a community innovation grant, based on the charity work we do with youngsters, and I just got the email that we were successful. I know we won't have the money within the next two days, but it would mean we can prove we have the funding."

Everything goes dead silent around us, like nobody quite knows what to say. This is amazing—this is incredible for us, but I feel speechless. Sapphy should be here. If she'd just waited.

"Why didn't you tell us about this?" Logan asks.

"I didn't tell anyone I'd applied for it because I didn't think we had a chance of getting an award in principle because they are really selective. Apparently they thought the idea was innovative."

Abs finally speaks after running a hand through her hair. "We have to let Sapphy know. How long has it been since she left?"

"About thirty minutes, maybe more?" I've already got my phone in my hand, selecting her number to call.

"Maybe we can catch her before she speaks to Maura and let her know. We can't let her walk in there empty-handed."

I nod my agreement with the phone pressed tightly against my ear.

Why couldn't I have convinced Sapphy to wait? Why did I give in so easily?

Her phone rings once, twice, and then my heart flutters.

"Hey," Sapphy's voice greets me and I feel so much better. I feel like I can exhale. Before I can speak, Sapphy's voice continues. "Sorry that I've missed your call. Just leave your name and number and I'll get back to you as soon as possible! Thanks!"

My heart falls. My breath strangles in my throat. Everyone is looking at me as I slowly lower my phone. "Just voicemail," I say, quietly.

My mind is now racing. Why didn't Sapphy answer? Is she already with Maura? If she is, how is it going? I don't know how to react...I feel defeated.

"Right, I'm going to try to catch her before she goes in. She bitched about having to wait to be seen by Maura before." Abs shrugged, grabbing her keys and phone. "Let's hope she's sitting in reception."

"It's going to be okay, Esha," Logan assures me.

I sit behind the desk, and Logan sits in one of the leather chairs. "I know," I tell her quietly. "It's just she should be here with us, not with *her*."

"In fact," Logan says. You can hear the smile in her voice. I look up to double-check that she is, in fact, smiling. "We should be getting the celebration ready for her to come back to. We've done it."

"You're right," I agree, feeling a smile tug up the corners of my mouth.

Logan's positivity goes a long way to making me feel better about the whole thing. I let the fact that she didn't answer my phone call melt off my shoulders. One by one they disappear and I find myself on my own. Well, I say one by one, but Maggie and Beth decide to head out for champagne and supplies, *together*.

It isn't until I'm sitting on my own that I realize how welcome it is. Everything has been so charged lately it's nice to have a moment to myself.

"Dani just messaged. She's just parking the car," Logan announces as she bursts into the room. I can't tell whether she is more excited at seeing Dani again or the fact she can share the good news.

She has barely sat down when there is a knock on the door.

We both turn to see Dani looking in at us, waving nervously. Logan gestures for her to come inside, and she steps in.

"What's going on here, guys?" Dani asks, a smile on her face. "Where's everybody else?"

Logan looks at her and she clearly lights up. Her fondness for Dani is obvious. She always seems to light up when she enters the room, or whenever they interact. "You'll never guess."

"Probably not." Dani laughs. "So just tell me."

Logan stands up from the chair where she was lounging, then walks over to where Dani stands. She reaches out and takes Dani's hands in her own. "Well, we just got the news from Beth...we have the funding we need!"

Dani's eyes open wide. She looks between me and Logan for a minute, as if she's trying to figure out whether or not we're telling the truth. When she realizes we are, a smile creeps over her face, stretching from ear to ear. "We do?! How? What? How?! This is amazing!"

"Beth applied for a community innovation grant and we just heard we've got it."

"I didn't even know she did that."

"Neither did we. She said that she did not wish to get our hopes up," I pipe in.

"That's great, but where is everyone?" Dani asks, looking around the room. "Shouldn't we be celebrating?"

"Well." Logan lets go of Dani's hand, then walks over to sit back in the chair she had previously occupied. "Sapphy went to see Maura just before we found out, so she still doesn't know. We tried calling her, but it just goes straight to voicemail. So Abs is now in hot pursuit of Sapphy to catch before she speaks to Maura," Logan said with excitement, "and Beth and Maggie have gone to get champagne."

"Damn, so Sapphy is still clueless and we're gonna get legless!" she says, then laughs at her own joke. "And Beth and Maggie have disappeared off together again…Beth never misses an opportunity. She only finished with her boyfriend a month ago."

"You don't think she finished with him for Maggie, do you?" Logan's eyes widened and Dani just shrugged. "What age is Maggie? Mid fifties?" She looked to me for confirmation and I let out a small laugh.

"Maggie is sixty-eight and proud of it." I know Maggie has no problem with me saying her age, and I have no doubt Beth knows too.

"Shit, but that's like years apart!" Logan exclaims.

"There's nothing wrong with an age gap," I remind her. After all, there is a decent gap between Sapphy and myself.

I hear Logan say something else, but it goes in one ear and out the other as my phone vibrates in my pocket. My heart flutters, excitement bubbles within me. It might be Sapphy.

I can't wait to tell her the news.

I pull my phone out and see that it's an incoming video call, but I don't recognize the number. I almost tap the red symbol to reject the call when I remember I couldn't get through to Sapphy's number. Maybe something has happened to her phone. Maybe she's had to borrow someone else's phone to call.

I answer it, expecting to see her smiling face—instead, I see the frame as if I'm looking on from a security camera. It seems to be an office. I'm confused. I'm just about to hang up when there is a crackle and I hear voices. One voice sounds like Sapphy. The camera adjusts to the direction of the sound and I can see Sapphy standing in front of a desk. She's talking to someone. My heart stops when I realize it's Maura sitting behind the desk.

As if against my better judgment, I turn up the volume so I can hear what's being said.

"You didn't waste anytime in getting here," Maura says without even looking up from laptop. The bad vibes that she gives off radiates through the phone, making a feeling of unease settle over me.

"I need to talk to you." Sapphy shoves her hands in her pockets. She's standing quite far back from the desk, almost out of shot.

"Oh, now you need to talk. After months of setting your geriatric pit bull on me, you now decide you *need* to talk to *me*?"

Maura's description of Maggie sends a ripple of anger through me. *Logan was right. That woman is a bitch.*

"What about me needing to talk to you, Sapphy? Or doesn't that count? You were desperate enough to call me when you wanted my money but let's be honest you were desperate to fuck me to get your hands on the investment you needed," Maura says, spitting out the words.

"Look, for what it's worth, I'm sorry. I know how it looked but..." Sapphy tries to reason, but Maura wasn't giving her the opportunity to continue.

"How it looked? More like how it was. You used me. You took advantage of me and then dropped me." Every word Maura utters is twisting the truth. "Does your precious Esha know the last time we met you gave me a massage? That your hands were on my breasts, offering me relief? I bet she doesn't."

My mind is racing. When was the last time that Sapphy saw her? Were Sapphy and I...? *Why am I seeing this?* A wave of nausea rises from the pit of my stomach.

"Maura, we both know it wasn't like that. We used to be friends. I don't want it to be like this."

"We used to be lovers," Maura whispers, walking around to the front of the desk and leaning against it. Sapphy doesn't move, but her discomfort is obvious in the way she stands.

"We've got near as damn all your money."

Maura seemed surprised and then amused. I don't want to watch Sapphy's discomfort; I didn't have the right to, but it was as if a morbid fascination holds me in its clutches, removing my ability to disconnect the call.

"Near as damn? What the hell does that mean?"

"We're short by about 2.5%. $138,000. It's a drop in the ocean compared to what you're getting." The defensiveness in Sapphy's voice is clear.

I should be there with her.

"When did $138,000 become a drop in the ocean? And let me get this right, you renege on the first deal, blank me and send in a minion to renegotiate, and now you have the audacity to demand a meeting to inform me you're coming up short—again? I said that if you wanted out of this deal; the deal which you knowingly agreed to, you had to pay me back one-hundred percent. Not ninety seven and a half percent."

I feel anger for Sapphy. Maura is impossible, and I don't know how somebody like Sapphy ever got wrapped up in her little game. I watch as Sapphy's hands leave her pockets, then ball into fists at her sides. Annoyance is clear on her face, but she takes a deep breath as though she is trying to contain her emotions before she continues.

"I realize that, Maura. I'm not saying you won't get the money, you will. But just let the cooperative go ahead and we'll be able to get that back to you, soon enough. I just want to give you the chance to—"

Maura laughs. "Give me a chance? Sapphy, what are you going to do if I say no? Do you really think I won't take over your little gym?" Her eyes narrow and it's like watching a hawk in flight focus in on its prey. "Do you want to finish your sentence?"

"Yes." Sapphy stands her ground. She looks at Maura, shaking her head. "I want to give you a chance to do the right thing."

I wonder if Maura was any other person, would she give in?

But Maura isn't any other person.

She cocks an eyebrow in Sapphy's direction before slowly shaking her head. "No, Sapphy, you're giving yourself a chance to look good again. I can sleep at night with the choices I've made. You're the one who can't. You're the one who regrets everything that you did. I've never forced you into anything other than keeping your word. Something you seem to find impossible to do."

Suddenly, I get it. I understand how she manipulates

Sapphy. How Sapphy for so many years fell for Maura's words, her twists and turns. The way Maura can distort the truth and pierce their armor with their own sense of duty is as sad as it is masterful. For the first time, I'm worried.

"Maura." Sapphy doesn't seem to budge. She stands her ground and I'm so very thankful. "I made that deal when I didn't know what I was doing. I was so caught up in what I wanted, in my dreams, and I was naïve. I'm sorry. I promised what I couldn't deliver, but I'm giving you everything I have."

On the video feed, I watch as Maura sighs.

"Okay. I accept your apology and thank you. It means a lot to hear you say that. You know, I always thought that you and I would end up together. We're the same, me and you, underneath it all. And we had some good times too, especially when it came to sex. You can't deny how compatible we are." She offers a small smile and Sapphy seems to relax and nod.

I shouldn't be watching. I don't want to watch. But my eyes remain glued to the screen.

"I want to help you, so I'm going to offer you one last deal. Say yes and you pay me what you have, you walk away, build your *cooperative* and get hailed a hero for having negotiated me down on price."

I see Sapphy breathe a sigh of relief, but I can't do the same. I don't trust Maura...I don't like the idea of a final deal even before I hear what she has to say.

Sapphy's head perks up, tilting to the side as she looks at Maura. "What is it?" she asks.

"Be with me one more time. Just for old time's sake. Let me finish all this up with a good memory."

That feeling in the pit of my stomach grows. I feel like I'm going to pass out or vomit. Maybe both. I focus my eyes on Sapphy, her response is all I care about.

Before Sapphy can speak, Maura closes the distance

between them, reaches out and places her hand on Sapphy's hip, gripping it firmly.

"Sapphy," Maura purrs. "I'm going to need an answer from you. I need you to tell me what you want from me. Do you want me to forgive the debt for just one last time?" She pulls Sapphy towards her. "Or do you want to continue this ridiculous fight we've been having for months now? One that you know I'll win."

I don't know what I'm expecting; Sapphy to push her away, or to tell her to back off. I'd take any of those responses, but Sapphy seems to be leaning into her grip on her hip, her eyes closing slowly.

She doesn't speak though…so I assume Maura seems to take that as a 'yes.'

She leans in, pressing her lips to Sapphy's neck.

I feel like I'm going to retch. Stomach acid rises, burning the back of my throat.

Sapphy, tell her no. Stop. Sapphy has to step away and end this. I wait for it, but it doesn't happen. Her eyes close as Maura's lips move further down her neck.

"That's what I thought. Good girl," murmurs Maura as she pulls back and smiles.

This can't be happening.

TWENTY-FOUR

"Esha?" Logan's voice breaks through the fog in my head, but I can't pull my eyes away from the screen in front of me. When I don't respond, she says my name again, "Esha."

I still can't pull my eyes away. "Yes?" I answer, my voice small and unsure. My chest hurts. Everything hurts.

"What are you watching? We're talking to you and you aren't listening. You've gone quiet."

I don't respond. It's just...I can't. I hear shuffling, out of the corner of my eye I'm aware of Logan coming towards me. Whether out of revulsion for what I am seeing or the shame I'm about to feel when they realize what I've been watching, I turn my phone around to reveal the screen.

Maura now has Sapphy pushed up against the wall, her hands exploring her body in ways that only I should be doing. The look of shock and disgust that crosses Logan and Dani's face likely mirror my own expressions. A stuttered silence weighs heavy as we all comprehend what it is we are party to.

"You shouldn't be watching that, Esha," Dani says after several seconds.

"I can't stop watching it," I say, turning the screen back around to face me.

It feels like an out-of-body experience. I feel like this isn't really my life. As if the body which Maura's hands explore is not the body I have worshiped with my own. Something inside of me breaks, cracks. I want to cry, but I can't. I just feel sick.

I lean back in the desk chair, trying to get myself to calm down. I can feel my heart pounding in my chest. Anxiety has made a home in the pit of my stomach, removing any capacity I might have had for rational thought.

Maybe the worst part is that I'm not angry with Sapphy... Sapphy, who could step back and stop this at any moment. I'm hurt, my heart is feeling like it's going to shatter...but I'm not angry with her. I'm furious with Maura, feeling like she's the monster of my nightmares, stealing away the one person who means the world to me. The one who holds my heart.

"Esha," Dani tries to speak, her voice soft and light, "you can't keep watching that. You need to turn it off."

I know that she's right, but that just feels impossible right now. I can't tear my eyes away, let alone stop watching completely.

Logan tries this time. "Esha, Dani's right."

I shake my head. "I know, but...I'm waiting for her to say no," my voice cracks, unable to contain what breaks inside me.

Maybe I've just moved on to denial. Moved from disbelief to depression, anger, and now straight-up denial. Logan's hand leaves my shoulder, reaching out towards the phone.

"Esha, you may get upset with me, but I promise that I'm doing this for your own good," she says.

Before she can end the video call, Sapphy speaks again.

"No," she says, her voice soft and barely audible.

On the screen, Maura pressed between Sapphy's legs, her hand sliding up the inside of her thigh. Right before it reaches her core, Sapphy's hand reaches down and clamps around Maura's wrist.

"No," she says again, this time her voice firm and decisive. Nothing like the soft 'no' from before.

"No?" Maura doesn't remove her hand; she just looks at Sapphy, clearly confused.

My heart skips a beat, the anxiety building to a crescendo. I'm faintly aware that Dani has come to join Logan behind me. Both are now watching over my shoulders as the scene plays out in front of me.

On the screen, Sapphy shoves Maura away from her, causing the other woman to stumble backward. "I said 'no'," she says again, her voice staying firm.

From the look on Maura's face, it's clear that she's not used to hearing that word. Especially from Sapphy. Her eyes narrow as she rights herself, trying to regain some composure. "Sapphy, I don't believe you know what you're doing."

Sapphy's arm is outstretched to ensure Maura keeps her distance. I see a flash of nerves cross Sapphy's face, but she inhales deeply and pulls herself up to her full height, and I nod, willing her courage because I'm sure Maura would jump on even the smallest weakness.

"I know exactly what I'm doing," Sapphy says. "I'm doing what I should've done from the beginning."

"Sapphia." Maura's voice is low, almost menacing. It sounds like a warning, and as soon as she continues to speak, I realize it is. "I need you to think about what you're doing. I need you to consider the choice you're about to make."

"I know what choice I'm about to make, Maura. It's the one where I finally tell you to back off."

Behind me, Logan claps her hands together, causing Dani and me to both jump and look at her. When we do, she gets a sheepish look on her face. "Sorry," Logan murmurs under her breath, a tint of red appearing on her cheeks. "I just...wanted to say that's my girl."

Anger is painted on Maura's face, but she's clearly holding it back, giving Sapphy another chance to say all the right things.

"Back off? Sapphy, haven't we already had this conversation? Don't you remember how this ends for you?"

"I know." When Sapphy speaks, the sadness and worry are clear in her voice. She knows what she's throwing away by speaking out here. My heart rate speeds up again. I don't want Sapphy to lose her dream. "I know exactly what's going to happen."

"So you know that I'm going to take your precious gym, right? Because we had a deal Sapphy—I've given you multiple chances, but you just can't pay up like you need to."

Sapphy stiffens. "Have you stopped to think about what all this says about you?" Sapphy shakes her head. "You're taking the gym because I won't sleep with you? What does that say about you? That you have to blackmail somebody to sleep with you?"

Maura looks like someone has slapped her and I feel the same emotions that Logan felt earlier. *Go Sapphy!* I'm so proud of her, although I realize what she's giving up to say this.

"Sapphy, I need you to think about what you're doing." Rage is now clearly building on Maura's face.

My heart is beating fast, my breath held fast as I realize I am now perched on the very edge of my seat.

"I know what I'm doing. I'm done. I'm not playing your games any longer. I've given you so many chances over the years to be a better person, but you never take them. All that matters to you—is you." Sapphy shakes her head like a disappointed parent with a naughty child. "Take the gym."

I'm stunned. Proud but stunned. Sapphy has just given away the thing that matters the most to her.

"Take the gym, Maura," she says, her tone even. "I've made excuses for you over the years. I've done my best to give you the benefit of the doubt, but I can't anymore. Take the gym because I've found something, someone that matters more."

Maura scoffs. "Is that what this is all about, Sapphy? Esha? You hardly know her. I give it three months and you'll be back here, telling me how sorry you are."

"That's where you're wrong. You don't get it. When you love someone, really love someone, then you'll understand." A look of sadness brings a shadow across Sapphy's face. "But I'm not sure you ever will. I love Esha, more than any boxing ring or punch bag or gym, and it has nothing to do with how long I have or haven't known her. With her I'm a better version of myself and that's all that matters."

Logan's hand is back on my shoulder, offering support. "Go Sapphy!" she shouts to the screen. "Atta girl!"

My heart feels full. Sapphy chooses me. At the same time, I can't imagine how awful this choice feels for her, and I hate she has to be in the position to make it. Behind me, Dani and Logan have fallen silent. We've reached a point where we don't know what to say. I think we all feel this simultaneous happiness mixed with sadness. Sadness for what Sapphy is giving away, but so, so happy that she's finally telling Maura exactly what she thinks of her.

"If you're sure—" Maura's words are interrupted by commotion behind them and raised voices seem to enter the room.

I gasp, as does Dani, as an irritated and out of breath Abs appears on camera.

"Sapphy!" Abs exclaims. "You don't have to do this."

"Miss Hearst, I'm sorry, I told her you were in a meeting but she—"

"I'll deal with you later," Maura snaps, radiating anger as

she dismisses her receptionist and then she turns her attention to Abs. "What do *you* want? Sapphy and I have already concluded our business."

"Abs," Sapphy completely ignores Maura. "It's okay. It's done."

"But it's not! We have the rest of the funding. It's all there, or at least it will be. We did it."

Sapphy seems confused. "We've got *all* the money? How?"

"Beth got a grant thing—it doesn't matter. All that matters is that we've got it." The grin on Abs's face was almost as wide as the room and unable to hold herself back, she launched herself at Sapphy, giving her an enormous hug.

"I can't believe it. We've done it." Sapphy's eyes seem to glint in the room's light and I realize she's crying. I want to be there to kiss those tears as they run down her cheeks. I reach out with my fingers to touch the screen, to touch Sapphy.

"You'll have your money, Maura, every cent as per our deal." I could hear Sapphy swallow down the emotion in her voice. "Do you want to come to the gym to sign the papers, or shall we meet at your lawyer's office?"

Maura's face is puce with anger. Slamming her hand down on the keys of her laptop, she screams, "Get the fuck out of my office. Both of you." And then the video call cut.

TWENTY-FIVE

SAPPHY

The drive back to the gym feels surreal. I'm not sure how to process what just happened. It all feels like an emotional blur. I feel so many things at once; relief that this whole sorry chapter is over; elation that together we moved mountains; *we have a cooperative*. There is even a little sadness that things had to play out as they did. I know most people won't understand this, but I hope Maura will, one day, meet someone who'll help her see the world differently. Someone who she'll love above everything else.

Most of all, I feel grateful. Grateful for everyone who has supported me. I have the most amazing friends who have stuck with me through it all. I only hope I can show them how much it means to me. But it is Esha who I am most grateful to, for allowing me to join her on what is an incredible journey.

I can't believe I walked in there, willing to give it all up. I can't believe that I was so ready to do all of that. To me, that speaks volumes about how I feel towards Esha. I knew before that I felt strongly, but now...now it's ridiculous how much I care about her.

I know I've never experienced love like this. I didn't even know it was possible to feel like this about anyone. There isn't any angst or drama, it's just so easy.

I pull up behind Abs's car. My hands are trembling. I don't know how to tell Esha everything that just happened. Abs knocks on the driver's window, pulling me from my thoughts.

I'm still muttering about how I can't quite believe everything that has happened as we step into the gym.

"Hi," Yvonne greets us from behind the reception desk. "They're all in there." She nods towards the front office and sure enough when I peer through the glass I see Logan, Dani, Beth and Maggie...and Esha. My stomach flips with nerves, or is it excitement? I can't be sure.

As soon as Esha sees me, she rushes forward and wraps her arms around me. I pull her close, inhaling her sweet musk. A warmth floods over me and my heart feels full. I clasp her, not wanting to let go. Everything is silent around us, between us. No words can speak louder than how right this feels.

It is the popping of a champagne cork that brings us back into reality and we pull apart, still unable to take our eyes off each other.

"I've so much to tell you," I say, and I can hear the waver of emotion in my voice.

"You don't need to. We heard everything."

Confusion washes over me. "How?"

Logan interrupts. "Esha got a live feed from Maura's office. Came through a video call from an unknown number."

"I don't understand?" I am completely confused. How could that even be possible?

"We think Maura has sent it. She must've been so sure you'd cave in and...you know." Dani shrugged. "But you didn't."

"Yeah, it was like watching a hero in a movie steal the day, like Rocky taking out Drago," Logan squealed, "or when Simba banished Scar from the Pride Lands."

Laughter bursts out across the room.

"Yeah, if anyone wants to join us for a quality movie night, then you're welcome," Dani says, then laughs. "Come on, let's get this champagne flowing. I'm parched."

While it had never occurred to me that Maura could do something so low, the more I thought about it, the more I realized I wouldn't put it past her. Her need to control everything, her need to control me was so great she'd have wiped $138,000 of debt to split up my relationship with Esha. I don't know if it's just desperate or tragic.

"I'm so sorry that you had to see any of that," I whisper quietly to Esha.

"I'm not. Not for a minute." Esha's smiles make my insides flip.

How did I get so damned lucky?

"To our new cooperative!" Abs cheered, holding up her glass.

"Our cooperative," we all cheered together.

"And to Beth," I lift my glass, "the woman who saved the day."

Beth smiled and on cue Maggie leaned in and kissed her cheek, setting it alight with a bright red blush, as we all cheered once again.

"Right, we should get everyone together and head out tonight to celebrate. Let's blow off some steam." It was more of an order than a suggestion from Logan, but everyone was quick to agree.

I'm not really in the party mood, I'd rather celebrate quietly with Esha, but Logan's right. We've all been through a lot this last six months, no, this last year and we did it all together so we should celebrate together.

"Fine, fine. We'll go out tonight." I grin, stealing a quick glance over at Esha to see if she's okay with it. She's smiling in my direction and I take that as a 'yes'. "And the first round of drinks is on me."

Grabbing Esha's hand, I lead her out of the office. The sounds of happy chatter fades we climb the black metal staircase. I just want a little alone time with her. I pull her to me and kiss her deeply as we enter my office, walking her gently back towards my desk.

"What are you doing?" Her eyes dance with a mixture of amusement and desire.

"I meant what I said today. Nothing matters more in this world to me than you." Before Esha can reply, I lean in and kiss her again. A hunger grows inside. I need her. I feel her hands pull me tighter, slide under my tank and press firmly against my bare skin. I step back and hook my thumbs into the waistband of her leggings and tug them down.

"What if someone comes up?" Her giggle is mischievous.

"They are all too busy drinking champagne to come up here." Discarding her clothing, I lift her onto the edge of my desk. Her lean, brown legs part and I kneel in front of her. My fingers glide gently up the outside of her legs. A girlish laugh erupts from her body as she tells me it tickles.

I press my face against the soft, firm flesh on the inside of her thigh and inhale. She smells sweet. Leaning back on her elbows, her legs spread wider across the clean, white expanse of my desk. Short hair, perfectly trimmed and shaped around her gleaming arousal, twitches in anticipation. My breath hitches, and my mouth waters. She is magnificent.

I hook my arms under her thighs and pull her to the very edge of the desk. I want to taste her, to allow my tongue to explore in small teasing flicks and long, languid strokes of pleasure, and that is exactly what I do. I bury my face deep into her wet center, coating my tongue in her juices. I take my time, taking as much pleasure as I give.

I ease my hands further round her thighs until her short trimmed pubic hair tickles my fingertips. I ease her lips apart and place the heat of my mouth over her clit, pulling her into my mouth. Her back arches but try as she might to squirm, she has nowhere to go; my grip is firm.

My tongue plays with her twitching bud, feeling it swell even more in my mouth. There is something so intensely satisfying in being able to bring someone to the very edge of losing control. I feel the weight of Esha's hands on the back of my head.

"Don't stop. Please Sapphy, don't stop," she begs.

Handfuls of my waves are clutched and pulled, which adds to my excitement. I want to make her come so hard, to make her gush in my mouth. Her hips thrust into my face, her hands jam my face into her, deeper still; I can hardly breathe, but still my tongue is relentless. Esha's moans grow in volume until an earth shattering scream fills the room, thighs clamp around my ears, and a spurt of desire trickles down my chin.

As her body recovers, tremors erupt through her body in bursts. Still kneeling between her legs, I watch her chest rise and fall as she tries to slow her breathing. She is sated, her body limp. Idly, I run my tongue over her core, licking away the abundance of moisture. She is slick and shudders once again at my touch. Slowly she raises herself and looks at me kneeling in front of her.

"I love you, Esha," I whisper.

TWENTY-SIX

The bass pounds through the floor of the club with such fervor that my cocktail shudders within its glass. We're all here, Esha too, who claimed to be too old when she heard the volume of the music from the street. But as Maggie reminded her, if the place was hip enough for her, then it was for Esha too.

Logan and Dani arrive with yet another tray loaded with drinks. There will be some sore heads at work tomorrow. Logan's in a blue button-up and a pair of jeans and Dani's wearing a blue dress that matches Logan's shirt. I have to admit that they're an adorable couple. Dani clearly makes Logan happy, and I'm so happy to see Logan thriving in a healthy relationship.

"I need to dance!" Abs announces, grabbing Hayley's hand.

"Abs, I've just sat down." Hayley's verbal protests didn't last long as she allowed herself to be dragged up to the dance floor.

"They are really going for it tonight," I shout across the table to Logan, as my head nods in the direction of the dance floor.

"Yeah, although Gracie has given them strict orders to behave themselves and not be too late home. I'm wondering which one of them is the kid." Logan laughed.

I looked over towards the throng of bodies which were all moving with the vibrating bass, but Abs and Haley had disappeared from sight. The club, Parade, which Abs had chosen for tonight's celebration, was busier than it would normally be for a weeknight, but that was largely because Logan had posted on the gym's social media account about our celebration and invited every member of the cooperative. In fairness, I don't think she realized this many people would come along to celebrate.

Esha's body is pressed tightly against mine as we're crammed into the booth, and every few minutes someone else comes up to congratulate us. 'How does it feel to be part owner of a gym?' is my reply because that is what we all are. Owners and winners.

I'm surrounded by people I love. People that matter to me; people that matter to each other; profoundly. I can't remember the last time I felt this happy, and a thought occurs to me, it's a mad thought but one I can't shake from my head. *What if I—?* But I dismiss it as quickly as it comes.

"Just ask her," Maggie shouts to Esha over the music, but Esha indicates for her to hush.

"Ask me what?" I'm curious now.

"It's nothing." Esha waves her hand dismissively.

"It can't be nothing. Come on, you have to ask me now." I see Esha flash an annoyed look across at Maggie, but I don't know why. Understanding I'm not about to give up, Esha rolls her eyes. "I was just going to ask you about the gym, perhaps offering some places to a charity I've been looking at. It helps young Asian girls who find themselves with no family support because of choices they've made. I thought we could make them feel like they belong. I know something like that would've helped me."

"Oh, right?"

"You seem disappointed. What did you think I was going to ask?" Esha cocks her head in question. I think I see the faintest smile on her face.

"No, I think that's a great idea." I place my hand against her cheek and lean in, placing my lips against hers. "I love your heart," I murmur when I eventually pull back.

The music changes, and Maggie jumps up out of her seat, causing everyone to look at her. "I love this one. Come on, who's joining me?" she asks, gyrating her hips and winking at Beth.

Within seconds we are all being dragged to the dance floor. I pull Esha in close to me and feel the warmth of her body against my own. I run my hands over the black leather pants she's wearing and something sparks inside me. As much as I am enjoying this night, I can't wait to get her home. When we can be alone.

I'm so lost in that thought, and all the feelings of longing that it brings, that I seemed to be the last person to realize the music had stopped. Everyone looks to the DJ in confusion. And then he hands a mic to Abs. Feedback crackles through the speakers and she cringes.

"Sorry. Most of you here tonight are here to celebrate Sapphy's and our new cooperative, and if you aren't, then I apologize. But look us up, it's Sapphygym.com, all one word..."

"Get on with it, Abs," Logan hollered.

"Right, okay, sorry. Well, I just wanted us all to give a huge thank you to Sapphy. It is your vision that has brought us all here and I'm so fucking excited—what?" Abs looked at Hayley, who I saw was mouthing something to her. "Yeah, right sorry for swearing, but honestly I want to say thank you to Sapphy because I never thought I'd be able to stand here and say I own a gym and I bet most of you didn't either. So please give it large, for Sapphy!"

My cheeks were burning as everyone cheers. I haven't done anything. Everyone here made the difference. I looked at Esha, who was grinning at me from ear to ear. Then the chanting started. "Speech, speech, speech."

I shook my head. This isn't my thing. I've no idea what to say...and then that fleeting thought entered my head again, and I seize it.

My smile erupts across my face and I walk towards Abs, holding out my hand to take the mic. I know exactly what I need to say, but even that certainty didn't stop my stomach from doing a backwards flip.

I take the mic from Abs and clear my throat.

"Thank you everyone, for coming here tonight to celebrate, for your support and belief in everything we are trying to achieve. The formation of the cooperative is just the first step for us, and I can't tell you how good it feels to have us all take the next steps together as a team. As my old coach used to say, there is no I in team and Sapphy's belongs to each and everyone of us. Everyone one is equally important as each other. Now, rather selfishly, I want to steal just a moment for a woman who is very important to me. My inspiration, my muse, and that is my beautiful girlfriend Esha. Now, I know all you non single people out there think you have the most beautiful woman in the world as your partner, but I'm here to tell you you're wrong and that's because the most beautiful of all is Esha, inside and out and tonight, Esha..." I inhale deeply meeting Esha's eyes. She really is the most beautiful woman I have ever seen. She smiles. A jolt of excitement courses through my body. There has never been a more right time.

"Esha, would you do the honor of spending the rest of your life with me as my wife?"

There are a few gasps, and excited oh's. I see Logan grab Dani's hand out the corner of my eye, but there is only one reaction I'm interested in, and that is the woman in the leather pants who is smiling and nodding and...who seems to be holding something out to me in an outstretched hand. As she comes closer, I see it's a ring.

"Yes, I'll marry you! You beat me to it." Grasping my left hand, she slides the ring onto my finger. "I was going to ask you."

Taking Esha in my arms, I kiss her deeply. Cheers of congratulations subside and the music volume increases as "Shut up and Dance" vibrates through the dance floor. But still, I don't let her go. I'll never let her go because this woman really is my destiny.

———

I can't stop smiling. Not at the club nor in the Uber on the way home. I have never felt happier. It's the feeling that fills every space in your body, starting in your heart and radiating outwards.

"I love you, Esha." I pull her close to me when we enter the bedroom. I have never been this vulnerable and open with anyone, and with her love it turns into courage. "Or will it be Mrs. Adamos?" I tease.

"I like the sound of that. Mrs and Mrs Adamos," she says to my surprise.

"Really, I mean you don't need to, it's a bit patriarchal the whole name thing..." Her finger on my lips halts my words.

"I want us to share the same name. I want us to share everything and besides, Esha Adamos has a beautiful ring to it, don't you think?"

I couldn't agree more.

Her arms are around me, hugging me tightly, and I return the embrace. Once again, everything we've been through today melts away. I have no worries about the immediate future. I know exactly where I'll be, where Esha will be. We'll be together because that's where we belong.

I lean in and press my lips to hers. This time I'm taking my opportunity. Without a second thought, I deepen the kiss. She eagerly accepts it, leaning further into me. Letting my hands lower to her waist, I walk her backward, navigating my way to our bed. I don't bother with lights. I know the path that I want to lead her down. The back of Esha's knees hit the bed, and she falls back with a soft bump. I crawl on top of her, continuing our kiss.

I just want to spend the rest of my night, and the rest of my life tangled together with Esha. I just want to continue kissing her until my lips are swollen and sore. I feel her hands wander along the curves of my body, and her touch tells me she feels the same.

I never expected this to be the outcome of my journey. I never expected to fall in love when I pursued my dreams. I never expected any of this, but I wouldn't trade it for the world. Every roadblock, every problem, only brought me closer to where I needed to be. It brought me closer to Esha, closer to my destiny.

Esha has taught me so much. She taught me it's okay to ask for help; she taught me I have the best support system in the world. Most of all, she taught what love can be. I never quite wrote it off, but I stopped chasing it a while ago. Esha changed all of that.

I break our kiss, taking a moment to look down at the

woman underneath me. I quietly memorize her features in the moonlight; the look of satisfaction on her face and how I feel being this close to her. I know that this is the love of my life and if today didn't break us, nothing will.

I smile as I pull her top up, revealing her soft brown tummy, and I lower my lips to kiss every inch of her beautiful skin. My hands make light work of the buttons on her pants, to show the top of sheer black lace panties. Sliding off the bed, I pull her pants with me, although it takes more tugging and squirming to loosen the leather than I expect. The delay does nothing to reduce our ardor. In fact, the casual intimacy of the moment brings us closer in playful laughter.

Naked, we dive under the covers, taking our time to stroke and tease. Light fingertip touches, the grazing of lips, warmth breath on sensitive skin, are all moments to be savored. There is no rush. We have all the time in the world and as we have already found out, our matching appetite for fun means we have hours of pleasure ahead before we succumb to dreams.

THANK YOU

Thank you for reading On The Ropes, I hope you enjoyed the book and if you did, I'd love it if you could leave a review.

If you would like to contact Ruby about this or any of her other books, she can be contacted at RubyScott.author@gmail.com

Alternatively you can sign up for her newsletter;
https://mailchi.mp/578501699a88/welcome-to-rubys

ABOUT THE AUTHOR

Ruby Scott was always an avid reader of #lesfic and lesbian romance and one day she got up had an extra cup of coffee and thought "I'm going to have a shot at writing a story." Her books, she jokes, are always a result of an extra cup of coffee. Born to a British parents, Ruby has lived in many places and loves travelling when it's possible. She never goes anywhere without her Laptop and her best pal, Baxter.

www.rubyscott.com

facebook.com/RubyScottLesficAuthor

twitter.com/RubyScottAuthor

ALSO BY RUBY SCOTT

City General: Medic 1 Series

Hot Response

Open Heart

Love Trauma

Diagnosis Love

Stronger You Series

Inside Fighter

Seconds Out

On The Ropes

Evergreen Series

Evergreen

Printed in Great Britain
by Amazon

61685000R00104